LORD OF ILLUSION

LEGACY OF THE BLADE SERIES - BOOK 3

ELIZABETH ROSE

ROSESCRIBE MEDIA INC.

Cover created by Elizabeth Rose Krejcik
Edited by Scott Moreland

ISBN-13: 978-1508715450
ISBN-10: 1508715459

Dedicated to my father, Stephen, the inspiration for my hero being a pigeon fancier.

Lord of Illusion – Book 3, of my **Legacy of the Blade Series** is near and dear to my heart for a very special reason. My father, born and raised in Chicago to immigrants of Slovakia, grew up in the poor part of town, and used to work for a man who owned pigeons. My father was his flyer – or the man who took care of the pigeons and flew them.

While writing this series, I had decided each of the siblings would have some kind of pet bird. In **Lord of the Blade – Book 1,** my hero has a raven he talks to that sits on his shoulder. In **Lady Renegade – Book 2,** my heroine is blind and her owl guides her. In **Lady of the Mist – Book 4,** my heroine is a pirate with a pet sea hawk.

Choosing pigeons for this book might seem odd but, actually, back in medieval times, courier, or carrier, pigeons were used to send messages quickly across the lands – in secret. People also raced pigeons for prize money. And I hate to mention pigeons were part of their diet as well, such as in pigeon pie.

While going through old photos from my mother's side of

the family, I came across three prize ribbons awarded by the Southwest Pigeon Flyers and Fanciers Association back from Christmas of 1920. It seemed another of my relatives was possibly a pigeon fancier, and though I have no records of which relative it was, I decided that I had to have my hero race pigeons as well. In the book, my hero grows up poor and has been raised to be a thief in order to survive. He starts raising pigeons, and one of them is named Homer. This name was created from both the fact these were homing pigeons, as well as because my father once had a pet pigeon named Homer.

This is the 3rd book in the series, and while they can all stand alone, it is always better to read them in order so there are no surprises ruined along the way.

Enjoy!

Elizabeth Rose

*"Our lives are just illusions,
and we are the masters of the dreams we create."*

DEVONSHIRE, ENGLAND, 1330

Gwyneth hurried through the courtyard quickly and quietly, her plump body jiggling with every step she took. One glance over her shoulder told her she had yet to be discovered for the horrible, unimaginable feat of treachery and deceit she'd just accomplished. Nightfall was upon her and she had to hurry. If caught, she'd be executed without a doubt and she couldn't say she didn't deserve it. Now, she had to get as far away from Blake Castle as fast as possible.

She hurried to the peddler's cart waiting for her return just inside the castle courtyard of the late Lady of Steepleton. One basket in each hand, she scurried up to the back of the open cart and slid them gingerly into the hay within. Her heart beat against her ribs harder than it ever had when she'd been out on one of her thieving excursions, trying to please her hard-hearted husband. But never before had she attempted to steal such valuable treasure.

"Let's go, William," she said in a hushed whisper to the boy driving. He was three and ten years of age. He turned his thin frame to look back as she climbed up behind him, leaning over from inside the cart.

"Did I see you with *two* baskets?" he whispered. "Oh, Cap'n will be impressed with the treasure you stole for him." His innocent brown eyes lit up, only causing her to feel a burning sensation in her chest. She hated the fact that William had to be a part of this treachery at all.

"Hush, before someone hears you. This is not treasure that *he* will want, but more for me."

Before the boy had a chance to respond, she saw the soldiers appear in the courtyard looking for her. They hurried back and forth, their cloaks billowing in the cool breeze as they detained the serfs and servants one at a time, asking questions and pulling hoods from their heads to check identities. All the while, they kept their hands close to the hilts of the swords mounted at their waists.

"Now go, anon, before we're discovered," she instructed the dark-haired boy. "We need to escape, before they close the castle gate for the night and we're trapped within."

William urged the horse forward. The wagon creaked with the brisk movement as it glided over the cobblestones. They made their way quickly under the gate, through the barbican, and over the drawbridge unnoticed. That's when the warning bell clanged from atop the tower and shouts were heard from within the castle walls.

"There is a thief among us," shouted a soldier.

"Close the gates," came another cry. "Lady Steepleton is dead and her babies are missing."

William's eyes opened wide when he heard the announcement. He turned toward the back of the open wagon to search her out.

"Please don't tell me there are . . . babies in those baskets."

Gwyneth didn't need to answer. The faint cries of two newborns split the air.

"Go!" she shouted from the back of the cart. "Before they hear the babes. Hurry!"

The boy slapped the reins to the horse even harder just as the soldiers noticed the cart already down the road from the castle. Gwyneth's heart raced as she peered through the darkness to see the sentry pointing in their direction.

"Take the path through the woods," she instructed. "'Twill be easier to lose them in the dark."

William did as she said. They could hear shouts from the castle guards in the distance and knew they'd been discovered. 'Twould be any minute now that the soldiers would follow in pursuit.

The wagon bumped as its wheels crashed over the uneven ground, and the baskets slid. Gwyneth moved quickly, managing to grab on to them and pull them toward her to secure them. Two sets of open eyes stared up at her from the babies. One baby had bright green eyes and the other had dark eyes, like a midnight sky. It was so unlike a newborn to have open eyes and to be looking directly at her. It was an omen, she figured. These children would be strong and determined.

"What did you do?" shouted the boy as he urged the horse

faster. "You were supposed to steal the lady's jewels, not her babes."

"She was birthing the babes and her husband thought I was a nursemaid so he sent me to the solar to help. Then, he left to go fight with the baron. Besides," she called over the noise of the wheels pounding on the hard ground, "this is better than jewels."

William stopped at the water's edge and jumped out. The boat they'd left was still there. The small vessel would take them to the fisherman's boat on the water, just leaving port. They'd be transported over the channel from Devonshire and back to Wales before the guards could stop them.

"You are addled to think Cap'n would ever accept babies over treasure. What he wants is coin, jewels, and power. Not helpless newborns."

"I've wanted a babe for so long," said Gwyneth, pulling back the blanket of the boy and examining the baby ring wrapped around the infant's wrist with yarn. In the light of the full moon, she could decipher an eagle with wings stretched out in flight engraved upon the precious metal. She knew she'd seen that same symbol fluttering on the flags from the castle's keep. The twin girl had one just the same.

"Now, I have a boy and a girl both," she said with a smile. "Before Lady Steepleton died from birthing them, she put these rings on them. Their father is gone and I heard he's being stripped of his title. And now, their mother is dead, so I don't see the harm in taking them. She didn't even have a chance to name them, so I will," she said proudly. "I'll name the boy . . . Madoc, after my Welsh grandfather. And the girl . . . since she was the second born and a repeat − I'll name her Echo."

"Let's go," said William, grabbing one basket while she took the other. They settled into the boat and he rowed quickly to the awaiting ship in the night. That's when they heard the castle guards shouting out and saw them waving their fists at them from the shore. If they hadn't had the babies, he was sure their archers would be firing at them right now.

"I fancy this one," Gwyneth said, pointing to the boy with the sparkling green eyes. "Though I will love both of them as my own."

"You are bewitched by wanting a babe for your own. Especially two! And we will hang by our necks when they catch us, for stealing babies of noble blood."

"These are the only babes I will ever have in this life," she told him, defending her decision. "My body has not borne the Cap'n a child after this long, and now I am too old. He should be pleased."

"Nay, he will kill you, if the castle guards don't kill you first."

They approached the fishing boat just as it started to pull away with a full crew and empty nets. A rope ladder was thrown down in preparation of their arrival.

"Arrrrgh," growled her husband, looking over the edge. "Hurry and get aboard. I hear the guards. You careless wench! They must know you've stolen their treasures." His dark, scraggly hair hung down around his shoulders. A tight cap covered the top of his head. His thick brows dipped in fury, and his upper lip curled to expose his crooked and rotting teeth.

Just as Gwyneth put her hand on the rope ladder, the babies both started crying at once.

"What's that I hear?" Her husband's eyes squinted and his mouth turned down into a frown, deepening the weathered creases around his lips. He tilted his head to see what the baskets down below held. "God's teeth! Those are babes, not treasures, Wife."

"Aye," she answered proudly. "One boy and one girl. Twins of the late Lady of Steepleton."

William picked up the boy, and she picked up the basket with the baby girl. Just as she was about to climb the ladder, it shot up into the air and out of her or William's reach.

"Husband, what are you doing? Drop the ladder before the guards catch me."

"I will not!" he exclaimed, giving command to the crew to raise the sails. "I won't have an army of soldiers after me for something I don't want in the first place. Such a worthless treasure, I will not be killed for."

"But we always wanted a babe," she told him. "Now you will have the son you always talked about."

"You said that when we took in William as an orphan from the gutters," he ground out. "And we can both see that he is as worthless as you."

"Please, Husband. These babes are all alone with no living parents. You could raise them as you see fit right from the start."

"Aye," he said, contemplating the situation, stroking the wiry beard upon his chin. "If I could teach them my ways before they are sullied . . . perhaps." He nodded his head and pursed his mouth as if he fancied the suggestion after all. "All right, then. Hand up the basket with the boy," he instructed. "Quickly. But I have no use for the girl."

Gwyneth's heart sank. He wasn't lowering the rope ladder

for her or William. And he didn't want the baby girl. She knew what he was going to do. He'd made his life pillaging off others, and wanted a son to whom he could pass on his vile trade. He'd never had any use for her even though she was his wife. And poor William hadn't the heart for the cutthroat life that lay ahead of him to be the son that the captain wanted him to be.

"Hurry up, Wife," he shouted. "I see the castle guards heading down the beach. We might be too far out for them to follow, but I will be out of here before they have a chance."

"What about me? And William?" she asked, holding her breath and waiting for his answer.

"What of it? You saw to it to get us into this mess, so see yourself out of it on your own. I'll have naught to do with either of you again. Now hand up the baby boy only, and I'll be on my merry way."

William started to raise the basket with the boy in it, but Gwyneth put a hand on his wrist to stop him. Instead, she traded William the basket with the baby girl and nodded for him to continue.

"Their names are Madoc and Echo," she shouted up to her husband. "And the baby rings are theirs so don't you be pillaging them for coin – it is the only thing they have left of their heritage. At least allow them that."

The captain lowered the ladder slightly and sent one of his lackeys to grab the basket that William handed him. Then, in a flash, the ladder snapped back up out of their reach. Her husband looked at the baby and gave a small nod, as if the idea of having a son pleased him after all. Then, without even a farewell to her or William, he disappeared onto the deck. She stood there wide-eyed as the ship sailed away from them, sealing their fates.

"You know he'll be after you when he realizes you slipped him the baby girl," said William.

"He'll never find us, I'll make sure of that," she said, settling into the boat and pulling the basket with the baby boy atop her lap. "Now, row out of here fast, and keep away from the shore. We have to fend for ourselves now, William. No one is going to help us, and no one is going to tell us what to do, ever again." She reached out a finger to the baby and his little fist grabbed it.

"'Tis just the three of us now. Just you and me, and baby Madoc." She chuckled and rocked back and forth on the seat. "I only wish I could see Cap'n's face when he discovers his treasure is naught but a girl!"

CHAPTER 1

DEVONSHIRE, ENGLAND, 1353

*M*adoc ap Powell sat at the trestle table in the great hall of Blake Castle, finishing off his meal of a tasty stew made from almond milk, clary sage, lots of garlic, and ginger. A seasoned meat with heavy herbs added not only texture, but flavor. A side of brown bread aided in sopping up the strong broth. He'd never tasted anything like it before, and it was delicious.

"Not bad," commented Madoc, wiping the bowl clean. "What is it?" he asked the fair-haired Sir Delwynn at his side. "Mayhap rabbit, or perhaps squirrel?"

"Nay," answered Sir Delwynn, picking up his tankard of ale. "I believe 'tis –"

He was cut short as a shout went up from the kitchen. A bird flew out into the great hall with a flutter of wings from overhead. It was followed by a hound, and Sefton, the kennel-groom, as well as Heartha, the castle's head cook.

Lord Corbett, the Lord of Blake Castle, and his wife, Devon, eyed them and then looked at each other in wonder.

"What is this all about?" shouted Corbett over the noise in the room.

"So sorry, milord," came Sefton's reply, trying to hold back the hound. "My hound brought in a bird, but it got loose before the cook could break its neck."

The bird flew around the room in circles. The women hid their heads while several of the knights jumped up on the long, wooden benches to try to catch it.

"Well, get the bloody thing out of here," instructed Lord Corbett. "I don't take kindly to my food getting cold in the midst of this commotion."

The bird landed on the table in front of a nursemaid holding a baby, and she screamed and jumped to her feet.

"That sounds like Rook," said Lady Devon, recognizing the cry of her baby. "Or mayhap it's Raven." She ran to the nursemaids holding their newborn twins, worried about the babies' safety as any protective mother would.

"Let me catch the fowl before it lands on the bairns," offered Storm, Corbett's Scottish brother-by-marriage.

Storm and his wife, Wren, were visiting from Hermitage Castle on the border at the lord's request. Corbett had recently discovered his long-lost sister, Wren, and they liked to spend time together to make up for the years they'd lost.

Storm cleared the dais table with one swipe, all the food and platters clanging to the floor. He then hoisted himself atop the table, putting out his hands, ready to trap the bird as it perched atop the iron circle candleholder hanging from the ceiling.

"God's eyes," bit back Corbett. "This isn't a competition, you fool! That was our dinner you just threw to the floor."

"Husband, get down from there," warned Wren. "Everyone can see up your plaid. Let me try," she suggested, and held out her hand, softly calling to the bird. She'd always had a connection to animals. Storm lowered himself to the ground, knowing she was the better of the two choices.

The bird flapped its white wings and headed toward her. But just then, Mools, their Scottish Deerhound, jumped up from under the trestle table snapping its jaws at the feathered intruder. The bird changed directions and headed back across the hall.

"Let me at it, milord," said a determined Heartha, waving her hatchet in the air. "It looks to be a good size and will fare well in tomorrow's sup."

"Nay, I'll have my fox hunt it down," boasted Renard, Storm and Wren's red-haired young son. He placed the fox on the floor and it zipped in and out between the legs of the castle's inhabitants who were now standing at the tables. Sefton's bitch barked and pulled away from him in chase of the fox instead. The dog was followed by Mools that obviously wanted to get in on the hunt.

Children screamed, babies cried, and men shouted. Women ran in a dither holding up their skirts trying to avoid the fox and the hounds. Then, Orrick, the old sorcerer, along with Zara, the gypsy woman, walked into the hall, confused by the commotion.

"Orrick," shouted Sir Delwynn. "Can you place a spell on the damned bird and strike it down?"

As the old man aimed his staff toward the bird, Madoc calmly got to his feet and held up a hand.

"Stop!" he called, his arm in the air. And to everyone's surprise, the white-winged bird went directly toward Madoc and landed on his hand. The hall went suddenly silent as everyone watched with open mouths.

"How did you do that?" asked Sir Delwynn in admiration.

"I didn't do anything," answered Madoc nonchalantly. "'Tis my bird." He carefully took the pigeon, cradling it in both hands and sat down at the table, noticing the piece of rolled up parchment attached to the bird's foot.

"*Your* bloody bird?" asked Sefton, hands on his hips. "My hound caught that, so that makes it mine."

"Nay," shouted Heartha, stomping over to the table. "'Tis me that'll wring the fowl's neck. We need it for the morrow's meal."

"I would never eat pigeon," said Madoc, running a finger over the bird's head gently.

"What do you think was in the stew?" asked Delwynn from his side.

Madoc looked at Delwynn who was smiling from ear to ear. His heart sank to think he'd eaten pigeon, especially since it was the best stew he'd ever tasted.

"I am sorry for the trouble it caused," said Madoc, excusing himself from the table, wanting to read the homing pigeon's message in private. Commotion started up again. Lord Corbett got to his feet and raised his hand above his head.

"Everyone . . . as you were." He looked to the gallery above stairs and nodded. "Musicians – a little music, please."

Madoc hurried to the corridor. Corbett, Storm, Wren, and Orrick followed.

"Dinna ye ken no' to bring a pet like that to the castle?" asked Storm.

"He could have been eaten," said Wren in concern, since she had such a love of animals that she wouldn't eat meat.

"What is this all about?" asked Corbett. "Madoc, I've not known you long, but the havoc caused by your – pet – is outrageous."

"Aye," agreed Storm. "Even when ye saved my life in the dungeon, ye were close to death yerself and ye didna seem so addled as now."

"I apologize," said Madoc softly, wanting naught more than to read the message, but not wanting to seem ungrateful for everyone's kindness. Lord Corbett and Storm both had been so grateful for his heroic deed that they more or less took him under their wings. "'Tis my homing pigeon." He didn't supply any more information.

"Homing pigeon?" asked Wren. "So it brings you messages from afar?"

"Aye," he answered. "Though 'tis odd I find it here since its loft is far from here in the hills across the channel. Something must have set it off course. I believe something must be wrong, perhaps with my mother."

"Then we'll leave you to your privacy to read the message," said Corbett, motioning with his head for the others to retreat.

Madoc hurried out to the courtyard, unrolling the parchment quickly. He walked under the light of a torch in the castle's outer wall to read the message. Four letters were scratched into the parchment A – N – O – N. He hurriedly shoved the message into his pocket and released the pigeon into the air. The bird would fly back to the loft being watched over by his friend, Owein. He needed to hurry.

Madoc turned on his heel but stopped as he was met with

the curious eyes of the old sorcerer, Orrick. "So, treasure hunter . . . where are you off to now?" Orrick perused him from the sides of his eyes. "You've visited often in the past six months, but seldom stay more than a day."

"I am needed at home."

"And where is this home of which you speak?"

"It doesn't matter," he said, stepping around the old man.

Orrick blocked his path with a step of his own. "And why do you have a homing pigeon when that is reserved for nobility only? There is something odd about you," he said. "Something that I cannot explain. I am sure you are not who or what you appear to be."

Sir Delwynn joined them just then, hearing the sorcerer's words.

"Aye, Madoc ap Powell, what was it you were imprisoned for when they found you in the dungeon? You never did tell us. Why were you in Hermitage Castle to begin with?"

"'Twas a misunderstanding," he replied, wanting naught more than to be away from here and the questions they were firing at him that he didn't want to answer.

"Wasn't it something about you trying to steal treasure from the earl?" asked the knight.

"Nay. I stole naught, I assure you."

"Aye. Well then, why not come back and join in the merry-making?" suggested Sir Delwynn with a slap to Madoc's back. "I, for one, have taken a liking to you. And I do believe Lord Corbett and Storm have also."

"I cannot," answered Madoc. "But please, give my regards to them all, and thank Lord Corbett for his hospitality. However, I must leave . . . anon. My family needs me."

"Of course," answered Sir Delwynn with a nod. "And Godspeed on your journey." He turned and headed back to the great hall.

"I see family is important to you," said Orrick.

"Aye. Now, if you'll excuse me, I must go." Madoc didn't look directly at the sorcerer when he spoke to the old man. It was almost as if the man could see into his life and Madoc didn't want to share that with anyone.

"Lord Corbett and Lady Wren recently found each other. They have two other siblings they've never known that were stolen by a nursemaid. No one really knows what happened to them, but word is that they died at sea."

"I am sorry for their loss. Now, if you'll please . . ." he tried once again to step around the sorcerer but was stopped by a hand on his shoulder.

"We will see you again," said Orrick. "But next time, it'll be with your family."

"Nay," he said. "Although I might return, my mother refuses to travel to these parts of Devonshire."

"Mark my words," said Orrick, looking into the depths of his eyes. "We will see you again – and with your family."

Madoc pushed away from the odd, old man and hurried on his way. He only had his mother, never having known his father. And William, though much older than he, was the only sibling he ever had. His mother had always told him his past didn't matter. And though he'd asked, he'd never gotten the answers he wanted. It seemed ironic that he never knew any information about his family and his past, and here was, a sorcerer acting like he knew all about his future.

Madoc knew the old man was wrong. His mother had told

him time and again she would never travel to Devonshire, even if her life depended on it. She hated the place for some reason or another, but Madoc had come to like it. So the sorcerer could not predict futures, after all, because never would Madoc be at Blake Castle with his family.

CHAPTER 2

*L*ady Abigail of Blackmore sat atop her horse as her entourage escorted her through the forests along the border of Wales. They were headed to Shropshire and she knew the Welsh marauders inhabited these parts frequently. She almost wished they would spring an attack on them, giving her the opportunity to slip away unnoticed. That's the reason she refused to ride in the wagon, insisting on riding her own horse instead. Just last week, they had been attacked by bandits, and if she'd had a horse instead of being inside the wagon, she would have been free.

Once again, she was trapped. She was being sent by her father to the vile Lord Lionel of Shrewsbury. She was naught more than a bargaining tool, sent to marry the man in order to set her brother free. Nearly a year now, her brother, Garrett, had been imprisoned by the man's late father and lord of the castle over naught more than jealousy. Abigail's father had stolen the man's betrothed, and their dispute had lasted over two decades. But now, by the hand of God – in the form of the plague – both her mother and the man were dead.

Both sides were being punished by God for their insolence. However, it was she who would suffer the consequences of her father's sins. One would think that with the deaths, this would end the dispute, but nay. Now Shrewsbury's son, Lionel, thought to benefit in the process. Before he would release Garrett from the bowels of the castle, she would be sacrificed. Her life was doomed, as she was promised to this man in marriage.

She loved her brother and cared about his return, but there was no way she wanted to be a pawn in their wretched game. Abigail was tired of her father's decisions and also tired of being a titled lady. No longer did she want to live by rules and be told what to do every minute of the day. She had run away from the castle several times this past month alone, and her father, Lord Oswald, had no more patience for her. That, in itself, was probably what finalized his agreement to send her away.

He decided she would be better watched after if she were married. Not to mention, after the disappearance at sea of her other brother, Edgar, a son to him was more valuable than a daughter. So he'd given her hand away in marriage and, as part of the bargain, included a very wealthy dowry as well. Of course, part of that dowry was already gone – stolen along the road by thieves just last week. Her entourage had turned back to the castle afterward at her suggestion. But now, once again, they headed for Shrewsbury with the dowry in tow.

She rode toward her doom, heading to the greedy man's castle against her will, to be his new bride. Thoughts ran rampant through her head of how she was going to dodge her men. She was well guarded, and the only chance she'd have was for a distraction, God willing, that would enable her escape and not threaten or take her life in the process. The last robbery had given them an excuse to go back home, but 'twas by her father's orders that, this time, they continue no matter what happens.

"Halt," commanded the guard from the front of the line. "There's a man down in the road."

Abigail's head snapped up, spying a prone man in a hooded robe on the ground. She couldn't see his face, just his grayish-white beard. Her eyes quickly searched the surrounding forest. This could very well be an attack – and, at the same time, her means of escape.

"What's happening?" she asked the guard next to her.

"There's an old man fallen in the road. He's probably just a peddler."

The guard at the front of the line lowered himself from the horse, looking to the trees, scanning the grounds. All the guards sat at the ready, hands on the hilts of their swords should they be ambushed again. Abigail watched as the guard up front walked to the man and leaned over to lend him a helping hand.

The man in the road hobbled to a standing position, grabbing on to the guard for support as he did so. He looked to be tall, but it was hard to tell since he was so bent over. Her heart sank. This was only an old man in need of assistance, naught else. Then, to her surprise, from where he sat she could see him pilfer the guard's pouch. None of the soldiers noticed, as they were too busy looking toward the forest for bandits.

"Many thanks, stranger," came the old man's crackly voice as the group continued forward. He then headed off quickly toward the woods. She couldn't believe what fools her father's men were and also how trusting they'd been. Was she really the only one who knew what had just happened?

"Stop him!" she called. The old man looked over his shoulder and sped up, running through the forest. She could see his horse hidden in the brush as the animal came forward to meet him. "Stop him, I say. Cannot you see that man just stole your pouch?"

They didn't hear her at the front of the line, so she turned toward the guard who protected her. "Go!" she commanded, "Hurry. Tell them what happened and go after the thief."

"Aye, m'lady," he answered, kicking his heels into his horse to move forward. She heard the shouts and saw the thief disappearing into the woods. This was just the distraction she needed. With not even one of her men watching her, she took the opportunity to head in the opposite direction and disappear into the foliage before they even knew she was missing.

She rode her steed hard through the woods, branches scratching her skin and tearing at her traveling clothes. Still, she didn't care. One glance over her shoulder told her she was yet to be followed. But when she looked a second time, a rider on horseback approached her, gaining on her quickly. In her carelessness, she misdirected her horse and it reared up, causing her to fall from her sidesaddle to the hard ground below. The rider came up behind her and she felt two strong arms pull her to her feet.

"Nay!" she shouted, pushing him away, "I won't go with you to marry that ogre."

Then she realized he wasn't a guard at all, but rather the old man in the road who'd robbed them.

"Let go of me," she cried. In her struggles, the man's hood slipped from his head. Though he had a beard and eyebrows of nearly white, the hair on his head was dark as a starless night.

"Hold still," the man ground out. A young man's voice slipped from his lips instead of the old, crackly voice she'd heard on the road.

"You are not an old man at all," she spat. "You are an imposter. Who are you?"

MADOC AP POWELL looked at the beautiful woman before him who was demanding his name as if he would really tell her.

"Who are *you*?" he asked in return.

"I am Lady Abigail of Blackmore," she retorted. "And I demand you release me."

"You, my lady, are the one who alerted the guards to my actions and almost got me killed." She was a feisty wench, he'd give her that. And twice as observant as any of the guards.

"They *will* kill you," she said. "Just as soon as they follow – which will be at any moment now."

"Nay, my lady. That is where you are wrong. For, at this moment, they are fighting off bandits who are headed in the opposite direction. I sincerely doubt they've even noticed you are missing."

"So you set up an attack and now you come for me?"

"I had naught to do with the attack. I work on my own. I just happened upon the opportunity before they did, that's all."

"Work?" she mimicked the word he'd used. "Hah. I sincerely doubt you have ever worked an honest job or day in your life. And to set things straight, I do not like to be referred to as an opportunity."

Once again, she was very observant, although he *had* worked at an honest job for a few years of his life. But he'd seen where honest work had gotten him when he'd ended up in the dungeon. Nay, what he did now was the better of the choices, and also what his mother had taught him to do from childhood.

He took a sheep bladder filled with water from his side and splashed it upon his face to rid himself of his disguise. The white powder in his beard and mustache washed out, leaving it as dark as the hair on his head. The powder in his eyebrows followed. He gave a sharp intake of breath at the coldness on his skin, then took a swig of the water and offered her some.

"Nay," she said, turning her head. As she tried to walk away, he realized her gown had caught on a branch.

"Well, Lady Abigail, I see your escape is foiled. You are caught not only by me but also by the guardians of nature."

"I wasn't trying to escape!" she exclaimed.

When she looked back up to him, he perused her beauty. A few years younger than he, she seemed to be, mayhap, one and twenty summers. Her hair was golden silk, spun from the faeries of the forest themselves. Her eyes were blue – deep blue – and clear like that of a midsummer's night sky. And her skin was alabaster and looked soft and supple.

"Well, I am glad to hear you were not trying to escape," he told her. "Because then you'll be willing to come with me when I return you for a reward."

He knew she'd never let herself be returned. He saw the desperation in her eyes. She was running. Of this, he had no doubt. And it wasn't from him. The determination on her face told him she would put up a fight before she ever let him take her back to the traveling party.

"They'll never give you a reward when you robbed them," she laughed. "You'll be thrown into my father's dungeon to rot."

His body tensed when she mentioned the dungeon. That was a place he'd inhabited more than once in his life, and never wanted to visit again.

"They won't know I am the same man once I change my clothes. Now, let me help free you."

ABIGAIL HEARD the man's words and a strange sensation went through her. Could he know how badly she wanted to be free? Away from her father, the guards, and her planned life and marriage to the vile Lord Shrewsbury? Here was a simple man, living his life how he wanted. There was no one to tell him what to do or who to marry. He had the life she so badly wanted.

His eyes interlocked with hers for a second and she found herself getting lost in the depths of the clear, bright green that shone forth from them. They were almost as green as the trees and plants of the forest. His face was very handsome since he'd washed the powder from his beard. And his build looked strong and sturdy from what she could see from beneath his long robe.

He reached to his waist and pulled out a dagger and started to cut her free. Then her eyes fell to the hilt of the dagger and the pink and green jewels embedded upon it.

"Where did you get that dagger?" she asked with a stiff upper lip, knowing he would lie.

"'Twas a gift from my father, milady. He gave it to me when I was just a child before he left for war across the sea and never returned."

She knew that was naught but a pile of dung. A man with no morals such as he could never have been raised by a fighting man who gave his life for his king and country.

"He gave you a lady's dagger with pink jewels in the hilt?" she asked, anticipating his next lie.

"Aye." He cleared his throat, obviously stalling to think up another wild story. He cut her free. Her hand snaked out, and she quickly grabbed his fist with the dagger in his grip.

"And I suppose your mother's name was Abigail and she died giving birth to you?"

He looked at her curiously as she put her hand over his. When he slackened his grip, she flipped the dagger over in his palm and pointed to her name scratched in tiny letters just under the hilt. She tapped her finger atop it. He squinted and moved closer to look at the engraving. She was sure he'd never even noticed it before now.

"Oh that," he said with a nod of his head.

"Do not even pretend that was your mother's name."

"Nay. My mother's name is Gwyneth. The dog's name was Abigail. My father knew how much the hound meant to me."

If she hadn't been so upset by seeing her stolen dagger in his possession, she probably would have laughed at the absurdity of his lie. She'd lost this precious piece in last week's attack. Now that she'd found it, she would not let it out of her sight again. It was by her late mother's wish that she even possessed it. Her father didn't want to waste the coin on her, but rather to spend it on her brothers instead. This was the last memory she had of her beloved mother and she would not let this thief take it from her.

"A master storyteller you are, but you make a horrible liar."

Before he had the time to answer, the sound of thundering hooves on the nearby road caught their attentions.

"That would be your entourage, my lady. So this is where I bid you farewell."

He pulled himself atop his horse in one quick move, turning a full circle to look at her one last time.

"Give me my dagger," she demanded, frantic that he was about to leave.

"I told you, my lady, 'tis mine."

He started to pull away when she stopped him again, reaching out to grab the reins from the side of his horse.

"Take me with you!" She needed time to think, and also to hide from her father's men. She didn't want to go with a thief, but it was the lesser of two evils considering where the guards would take her. Besides, she couldn't let him leave before she had a chance to claim her dagger. He seemed to consider it for a moment, but then shook his head.

"As comely as you are, 'tis tempting. But I told you, I work alone." He reached down and removed her fingers from around the reins. "I do not need you slowing me down, nor do I need an army of angry English soldiers on my tail. So, nay, I cannot do that."

"You must."

He smiled a crooked smile and glanced back toward the road. "That is where you are wrong, my lady. You are the one who must do as told, not me. I don't know what it is you are running from, but I wish that I could help you. But alas, I travel alone. Now, once again, I bid you farewell."

With that, he kicked his heels into his horse and headed deeper into the woods toward the Welsh border. Abigail could hear the guard coming to claim her and she wasn't happy. She'd almost managed to escape. If only this thief had helped her, she'd be far from here by now. Instead, she would continue to head to her doom while he rode away with her last memory of her mother strapped to his waist. She knew what she had to do. And she had a feeling it wouldn't be long before she saw the mysterious stranger again.

MADOC WAITED IN THE TREES, hidden far from the single guard who'd come to claim her. But he was still close enough to make sure that Lady Abigail was collected by her father's man and not the group of bandits. He fingered the jeweled dagger at his side, feeling like a simpleton for never noticing the name engraved upon it when he'd stolen it just last week from the thieves he'd once worked with. Now he knew where they'd pilfered it. And they were the same ones that just attacked her little traveling party again, he was sure of it.

The thieves were on his trail, and getting closer. He always had to stay one step ahead of Gruffydd and his men. Because of his betrayal to them, he'd hate to think what they'd do to him if they ever caught him.

Now, he almost felt bad about what he'd done, and also for the fact he just left Lady Abigail there when he had the means to help her. Her longing to be free of the life she lived cried out to him so loudly he had a hard time ignoring it. He knew it well, since he'd been hearing it in his own head for quite some time now.

He was no longer sure he liked his life either. They had so

much in common, even though she was a noble and he was only a common thief. He could see in her eyes that she yearned for what he had. He knew he was correct after hearing her say she wouldn't marry the ogre, and also by the fact that she was trying to escape. After his stay with the good people of Blake and Hermitage Castles these past few months, he had a longing in him, too. He wanted to be free of living as a thief in the night.

Instead, he wanted to live as a titled man and in a castle with rich food, cheery music, and fine maidens for the taking. But that was only a dream. People like him had no right to even imagine living a life like hers.

It was ironic that they should find each other in the woods, both trying to escape who they were. And it was even more ironic that he should have *her* dagger at his side. He knew she wouldn't give it up this easily. Nay, she would try again to retrieve it. He was sure he'd find her in the woods, escaping again, before this was all over.

CHAPTER 3

*M*adoc rode up the Black Mountains, deep into the wilderness of Brynmawr, just over the Welsh border. His concealed home lie just ahead. He hadn't been back now in a sennight, and only hoped everything was in order with his birds. When he'd left for Devonshire, he'd paid the old sheepherder, Owein, dearly to tend to his pigeons until his return.

Owein had been a friend of his for the last several years, ever since Madoc built this place with his own hands, right after he escaped from the dungeon of Shrewsbury. Owein had kept Madoc's secret life to himself, never asking questions, and Madoc respected that and did the same for him in return.

It was peaceful living in the hills and away from everyone. But lately, he was feeling the need for companionship. He hadn't bedded a woman in some time now. And now that he'd met Lady Abigail, he couldn't get the thought of her out of his head.

"Owein!" he called, spying the man's sheep grazing in the hills. He should be here somewhere. Madoc let him use his house while he traveled, and Owein appreciated it, as the nights were cold.

"Owein, I've returned!"

He could hear the cooing of his birds as he approached. He kept wondering why Homer, his favorite carrier pigeon, had flown across the channel instead of coming back to the loft earlier. She had flown many times before from his loft in Shrewsbury to here, and knew where to go. Something must have upset her to make her fly off course and get lost. He'd trained his pigeons well over the years and knew they were fast and accurate. He'd learned everything about birds from working in the mews at Shrewsbury Castle years ago.

Pushing his way into the little hovel of wattle and daub, Madoc found Owein lying in a heap on the floor, moaning. Dried blood caked his face. The cuts upon his gnarled fingers looked as if he'd been hit.

"God's eyes! What happened?" Madoc ran to him and helped him into a chair. Then he grabbed a rag from the counter, dipping it into the basin of water and proceeded to cleanse the man's wounds. A purple stain encircled one of Owein's cloudy blue eyes, and another bruise was visible on his swollen jaw.

"Madoc, thank God ye returned. I didn't tell them anything, I swear I didn't."

"What do you mean? Who was here?"

"They were here looking for ye. They're on to yer deception. Mad they were. So mad I thought they were going to kill me."

At first, Madoc thought Owein meant the guards. But realizing they would never travel up here in pursuit, he knew it had to be the bandits who did this to the poor, old man.

"Was it Gruffydd and his men?"

"Aye. They were spouting something about a missing jeweled dagger that ye stole from them."

And that, he did. While they slept, he'd crept into their camp, taking what he needed and wanted, and feeling no remorse. He'd once been a member of this group until he almost ended up dead in the dungeons of Hermitage Castle thanks to them. Had he known at the time his thieving would put him under the control of their leader called Cap'n, he never would have joined them.

He'd never met their infamous leader who he knew was naught but a pirate, nor did he want to. When he stole something, it was for his purposes alone. He'd traveled with them for less than a month, but that was long enough to know he wanted out. For months now, he'd been on his own and wanted naught to do with them ever again.

"What did you tell them Owein? Didn't you tell them I was dead?"

"Aye, I told them ye perished in the dungeons of Scotland, but they didn't believe me. They wondered how I would know. Besides, when their treasures went missing, they knew only ye could steal from under their noses and not be caught."

"I am sorry old man for the trouble that I've brought you."

"Nay, don't be. I have enjoyed yer conversations and it does my heart good to help ye, Son."

"Are the birds in good order?"

"They are. But one of yer messenger pigeons came in just as they attacked me. It got frightened and flew off over the water."

"Bloody hell, how long have you been lying here?" asked Madoc, knowing it had been a full day since he'd gotten the message. "The homing pigeon found me. With it was an urgent request to return home. I believe my mother needs me. Her health hasn't been stable for quite some time now."

"Then go," he said confidently. "I will be fine. The thieves won't be back this way, I'm sure. They headed north."

"Aye, I believe I've encountered them on the road just recently. 'Twill be dark soon. I will leave at first light." Madoc pulled the pilfered pouch of coins from his side and threw it on the small, wooden table in the center of the room. It landed with a thump and a jingle. "That should be enough to take care of you and your son, and feed the birds until my return. If you need me, just send out one of my best flyers."

"Ye know I can't write or read to send ye a message."

"You don't have to. I know each of my birds like the back of my hand. If I see any of them roosting in my pen in Shrewsbury, I will know you called for me and return anon."

"But what if ye send a flyer here? What shall I do with the message if ye need help?

"If a message comes by pigeon here, somehow get it to Lord Corbett in Devonshire. If I send a message, 'twill only be because I'm in another dungeon and need an army to get me out."

"Will do," he said, rubbing his aching head. "I wish that I could travel to Devonshire myself. But if need be, I'll get my son, Hadyn, to take it there, I promise."

"Hopefully, I won't need to take you up on your offer."

"Well, I've got sheep to tend," said the man, getting to his feet. He scooped up the pouch of coins and fastened it on the rope belt at his waist. "I will be back in the morning. I will head home for the night for fresh clothes and to tell my son the plan." Owein left over the hills.

Madoc removed his cloak and went to his pen to check his flock. He'd constructed a wooden building at the back of the house and that is where his birds roosted. The open windows were covered with thin, wooden slats to allow airflow but keep out predators as well as keep the birds inside. A small hole in the roof sported a trap door. When a messenger bird returned, it dropped into the loft for food, but could not get back out. He'd spent many hours training each bird and hand feeding them ever since they were squabs.

Madoc opened the door to the small building, ducking to enter. Inside, the ceiling was high, allowing the birds to fly about. His eyes got accustomed to the dimness and he went to the corner, opening a barrel and scooping out seed and grain for the birds to eat. They flew around his head, acting very hungry. Afterward, he filled their water and checked on his breeders sitting on their eggs. There were no young ones yet, but they should hatch soon.

He had about thirty birds here and the same amount in his pen in Shrewsbury. He looked up to the roost and noticed Homer, his favorite hen. He was happy to know she'd made it back to the loft after delivering her message to him at Blake Castle. She had always had a connection with him more than the rest. She was a big, white bird with black tail feathers. She fluttered down to greet him. Madoc smiled and ran his fingers over her soft head in a mock preening that she loved.

"My many thanks for your fine service." She cooed and puffed out the feathers on her chest, liking his attention even more than the rest. Then he raised his hand quickly into the air, sending her back up to the rafters.

The birds were noisy which meant they were not only hungry but also happy to see him. His pigeons had an inbred knowledge to always find their way back home. For some reason, even though Madoc's true home was in Shrewsbury, he kept finding himself returning to Devonshire and Blake Castle. He liked it there. And oddly enough, since he'd met Lord Corbett and the others, the castle almost seemed to him like home.

Lord Corbett offered to let him stay at Blake Castle. The lord's sister, Wren, also offered him her home in Scotland, since he had saved her husband, Storm's life in the dungeon of Hermitage Castle. Madoc wanted more than anything to stay with them, but couldn't. He had to go back to his mother and William. It had been too long that he'd ignored his birds in Shrewsbury and he didn't feel good about it. It was a lot of work to house birds at two different locations. Thankfully, his brother, William, helped him on the other end. William was quite a bit older than Madoc and not a blood brother, but the only sibling he'd ever had.

Madoc had been training his birds for the pigeon racing competition being held in Shrewsbury soon. His birds were fast and he knew he had a good chance to win the prize money. It would be enough for his mother and William to live on, as well as enough to feed and care for all his birds for a whole year.

He picked up one of the smaller birds, a dove. 'Twas one of the prettiest in his opinion, pure white like a snow-covered mountain. He ran his finger over its back. It pained him to think that once he entered the competition, his home here would no longer be a secret. Still, to win the prize money would take the worry from his mind, knowing his family would be cared for.

All of a sudden, his birds seemed to sense something. They

flapped their wings and flew around the pen, noisier than usual. Madoc's head snapped up as he looked around and listened. His birds were perceptive and had often alerted him to a predator or even an approaching stranger before they arrived. In two long strides, he was at the door. He slipped outside quietly with his hand on his dagger as he scoped the grounds. That's when he noticed that the door to the house was ajar.

Since Owein had already left, he hoped Gruffydd hadn't returned. The sun was setting in the mountains and cast a deep shadow over the land. He made his way silently over the damp earth and stopped and rested his hand on the door. Then, in one swift motion, he pushed it open and stepped inside.

ABIGAIL SCREAMED as an arm grabbed her from behind, and the sharp blade of a knife pressed against her throat. The hood of her royal purple traveling robe hid her view of her attacker, but she could feel a hard, warm body pressed up against her. Then a deep voice ground out in her ear.

"Who are you and what do you want?"

"I . . . I . . ."

She didn't need to say more before her attacker dropped his arm from around her and lowered the blade from her throat. Then, two strong hands grabbed her by the shoulders and roughly turned her to face him. He quickly lit a candle, and a soft glow encompassed the small room.

"You!" said the man from the woods she'd met earlier.

"You!" she echoed him, her eyes settling on her dagger in his hand.

"Do not tell me you followed me here for this?" He held up her stolen dagger that shone in the firelight.

"You had no right taking it from me in the first place."

He shook his head and looked at her as if he couldn't believe she was there.

"I told you . . . I didn't. Actually, it was bandits who stole it from you. I just lifted it from them." He smiled as if the thought amused him, causing her to want to slap the smile right off his face.

"That doesn't make thieving the right thing to do."

He almost seemed to consider it for a moment. Then, he slowly went and closed the door.

"Well, Lady Abigail, it looks as if you'll be leaving here without the dagger. However, since 'tis already dark I can't let you go until morning. 'Twould be too dangerous to travel in the dark on this steep, rocky terrain. How did you get here by yourself? I didn't see a horse."

"'Tis there," she assured him. "It's in the woods, tied to a tree down the hill. It was . . . tired," she added, then cursed herself for saying something so stupid.

"I highly doubt the horse was tired, but I would be willing to bet you are. And 'tis more likely you didn't want me to know you'd followed me and came to steal my dagger. That's why you hid the horse." He plopped down on the straw-stuffed mattress in the corner and pulled off his boots. One after the other, he threw them to the center of the room. "How did you escape the guard?"

"I hit him over the head with a branch, so hard it knocked him to the ground," she admitted proudly. "Then I stole his horse, knowing he wouldn't be able to ride mine with a sidesaddle to follow me."

"Impressive," he said, running a hand over his short beard. "You'd make a good thief, if you ever wanted to change professions."

"What did you say your name was?" she asked, sitting on a chair by the table.

"I didn't." He leaned back on the pallet and put his arms behind his head. "Good try, but you're going to have to work on your subtlety. Now, tell me what it is you really want, my lady. If I could guess, I'd say you were running away from a life you don't like."

"And if I could guess about you, Thief, I'd say you were unhappy with your life. That's why you use a disguise to be someone else as you help yourself to coin you haven't earned and weapons you don't know how to use."

That was the wrong thing to say. His eyes turned dark, and he pushed up slowly from the sleeping pallet. Then, in one move, he gripped the dagger and flung it through the air. It whizzed right past her as it twirled end over end, finally embedding itself into the wooden door.

"Do not assume you know anything about me," he told her.

"Well, Thief, if you won't tell me anything, then I'll assume what I want."

"And stop calling me Thief."

"If you want me to do that, then give me a reason, and tell me your name."

"I'll tell you nothing since you're only going to run back to your father and have me thrown in the dungeon for stealing your dagger. After all, that is why you followed me, wasn't it?"

"Nay." She looked down to the ground and bit her lip. "Actually . . . you were partially right. I am running from a life

I don't like. But I have no intention of turning you in. That is, if you'll help me," she added quickly.

He lay back down and closed his eyes with what looked like a sigh of exhaustion or, mayhap, relief.

"And what is it you need me to help you with?" he asked with his eyes still closed.

"I need a place to stay for a while. And a disguise. You seem to know all about disguises. And this house is pretty well hidden, so this should work fine," she said, perusing the small abode.

He chuckled, making her wonder what he was thinking.

"So who is this ogre of a man you are to marry?" he asked.

"How did you know about that?"

"You told me . . . when you thought I was one of your guards in the woods."

"Oh. That's right. The man I am to marry is the Lord of Shrewsbury. He is said to be ugly and fat and very greedy."

"Shrewsbury?" he asked, sounding suddenly interested. His eyes popped open and he partially sat up on the bed. "I see."

"So, will you help me or not?"

He shook his head and lay back down. "Well, I'd love to, my lady. But you see, I am leaving on the morrow."

"Then I will go with you. Your life seems exciting. I will travel with you in disguise and do what I want when I want. I like that idea. So then, 'til the morrow."

His eyes were closed again and, for a moment she thought he was asleep. She looked around the room and at the empty shelves, not seeing any food or ale. The mattress he reclined on and the chairs at the table were the only places to sit. "Where shall I sleep?" she asked.

"Wherever you want," he answered.

"But you are using the pallet and this chair is uncomfortable."

"If you'd rather, you'll find soft straw out in the loft with the flock."

"I'll use the chair, thank you," she retorted. "And do tell me, where are we off to on the morrow? Perhaps up the mountains or over the sea? Or mayhap to a fair in the Highlands to watch the fierce Scots compete?"

"Nay. I'm sorry to tell you that we're not going anywhere nearly that exciting. I am headed for home in the morning to see my mother."

"All right then." She nodded. This wouldn't be that bad. It might be nice talking to another woman. "So, where would that be?" It felt exciting to be starting her journey and going anywhere but to Lord Shrewsbury's castle was fine with her.

"Shrewsbury," he told her, never opening his eyes.

Her mouth fell open and her heart sank. That was the last thing she wanted to hear. Now, she'd have to spend the rest of the night planning her next escape.

CHAPTER 4

*M*adoc awoke to the sound of voices outside his window. The sun was already rising, sending its weak rays in through the window. He couldn't believe he'd slept so late. He had wanted to get an early start to Shrewsbury and was already behind schedule.

"Take your hands off of me," he heard a feminine voice say from outside. He'd almost forgotten the troublesome wench had let herself into the house last night. He hurriedly pulled on his boots and made his way across the room. Of course, he wasn't surprised to find the dagger no longer embedded in the wood where he'd left it.

He pulled open the door just as Owein was reaching for it from the other side. The man held on to Lady Abigail's wrist with one hand and gripped the dagger in his other. His son of seven and ten years held on to her horse's reins as he brought the animal toward the house.

"We found her sneaking out of the house and down to that horse in the woods," said Owein. "And she had yer dagger on her. I brought the thief to ye right away."

"Me a thief?" she asked and laughed. Then she glared at Madoc.

"Thank you, Owein." Madoc took the dagger from him and fastened it to his waist belt. "And thank you as well, Hadyn." He nodded to the man's son.

"My pleasure," said Hadyn. "I'll be off now to feed the flock before I tend to the sheep."

"Aye," answered Madoc.

"What do ye want me to do with her, Madoc?" asked Owein, looking the girl up and down. "She is not dressed like a peasant. And by the looks of her smooth hands and fair skin that have barely seen the sun, I'd guess she's someone of importance."

"And your guess would be correct," said Madoc, taking Abigail's wrist and pulling her into the house. "Just keep it to yourself, good man, and all will be well. We'll be leaving anon for Shrewsbury."

"I told you, I'm not going to Shrewsbury to marry the lord of the castle," she complained.

Madoc grimaced at hearing her words. Now Owein knew more than Madoc had intended on telling him. He had planned on being long gone before Owein and his son showed up. But now there was no hope for that.

"My lady," Owein said with a bow. "I am sorry, I hope I didn't hurt ye."

"I am Lady Abigail of –"

"Thank you, Owein," said Madoc, closing the door and pulling Abigail over to the table. "What do you think you are doing announcing your presence here? If you are on the run, you don't boast to common sheepherders who you are."

"Well, at least I am not afraid to tell someone my name . . . Madoc!"

"Damn," he cursed under his breath. Now that she'd heard Owein say his name, she'd most likely be announcing it everywhere they went.

"Let's go," he told her, taking her by the arm. "And try to refrain from talking on our travels if you will." He grabbed his cloak and made his way out the door. Dragging her along with him, he headed to the horses where Owein was filling the travel bags with food and ale for the trip.

"Will ye be wanting extra provisions for Lady Abigail of . . ." Owein stopped and stared at her.

"Blackmore," she answered, flashing a daggered glance to Madoc.

"Nay, we'll be on our way," Madoc told him, mounting his horse, eager to leave. "Damn," he spat, remembering he needed to set his flyers free so they'd return to Shrewsbury – their home. They needed exercise and practice flying over longer distances if he was going to win that race.

He had five of his flyers housed here now, and there were five more in Shrewsbury that belonged here. The birds would only fly one way – to return to their roost. This enabled him to maintain a method of communication. The rest of the birds lived here, and that ensured control that they wouldn't fly away once let out of the pen.

He walked into the loft to find Hadyn just finishing up cleaning the pen. To his left were his breeders. The main room was an indoor fly area for the birds. Most of the windows jutted out into an outdoor area, but were still enclosed by the wooden bars. This enabled the birds to get fresh air and sunshine while housed.

There were dozens of perches at every level filled with birds of various colors. The males had brighter colors than the hens. He had pigeons of all kinds. Some were gray, some tan or brown, some a shade of orange, and some were white. They ranged from having multi-colored heads to stripes on their wings, to plain white, like his snow-white doves.

"Make sure to let them all out to fly during the day," he instructed Hadyn. "They won't go far – except for the one I'll leave in the side pen. That one stays put or he'll go back to Shrewsbury. I will leave him here in case we need to communicate."

Madoc entered the far right pen, scooping up one of the birds before opening the wood-slatted window and letting his flyers go. He then closed the window and returned the single bird to the pen, isolating it from the rest of the flock to ensure it wouldn't fly away.

"Aye, I will, Madoc," said Hadyn with a nod of his head.

Madoc looked up at his pigeon, Homer. "I can't take you with me this time, but I will be back for you soon." He hurried back outside to find Abigail with her hand over her mouth, looking up to the sky with a terrified expression on her face.

"Oh!" she exclaimed, watching as two of his flyers rolled and dived and somersaulted in the air as if they were shot and then dashed back up to the sky.

"They're my Rollers," he explained. "They like to show off."

He mounted his horse. "Owein, I left one bird in the side pen. Send him out if there's a problem or if the squabs are born before I return. Either way, I'll come anon if I get the message."

"Aye," answered the man, holding out his hand to Abigail. "May I give ye a lift to yer horse, my lady?"

Abigail glared at him and all but pushed him out of the way. Slipping her toe into the stirrup, she pulled herself into the saddle. Madoc thought she looked amusing sitting astride with her long gown. He was sure she wasn't used to this kind of saddle and knew she would slow him down.

ABIGAIL FOLLOWED CLOSELY behind Madoc on the trip as he took off through the woods at a good clip. She had half a mind to refuse to go with him, but she was sure he wouldn't care one way or the other and leave without her. Besides, she didn't want to stay behind. She wanted to go with him. He intrigued her, crude as he was. He lived an exciting life and, perhaps, would take her on an adventure. Anything would be better than going to Shrewsbury but, unfortunately, that's exactly where he was taking her.

"Can we stop for a minute?" she shouted, her body aching from riding astride. She wasn't used to this, although it did make travel faster.

"Can't do that," came his reply from ahead of her. "If you're going to tag along, you need to keep up with my pace."

Tag along? She really didn't like that comment. Although, she supposed, it was exactly what she was doing. But in all her years of living at the castle as a lady, she'd never had to put up with such disrespect. Therefore, she would show him who was tagging along, and it wasn't going to be her. She dug her heels into the sides of the horse and covered ground quickly. Directing the steed with ease, she came up next to Madoc at a full gallop.

"Don't ever say I'm tagging along," she warned him. Then with a slap of the reins, she shot forward, leaving him in her dust. She laughed to herself at seeing the expression on his face. It obviously wasn't something he expected. Abigail continued on, never slowing or looking back to see if he followed. Spent and exhausted, she spied a little inn at the crossroads and decided to stop there to wait for him.

In her hurry to outride Madoc, she'd been careless. If not, she would have noticed two horses draped in her father's crest and trappings tied up at the post out front of the inn. The first thing she had done after stealing her guard's horse, was to rid herself of any identifying pieces with the crest of her father. Too late, she'd spotted them, just as the door to the inn burst open and two of her own guardsmen, Desmond and Emric, walked out.

"Lady Abigail!" cried Desmond, rushing to her side. She turned her horse but it became skittish.

In the mere moment it took to calm it, Emric grabbed the reins. "Stop running off or your father will have our heads."

"We've been looking for you," Desmond growled. "Now let's head back before it gets dark."

With a quick glance over her shoulder, Abigail hoped for the thief to come to her rescue, but he wasn't there. Why should she be surprised? He probably was off lifting a pouch or swindling an old woman. She shouldn't have expected a heroic act from a man like him.

"Nay," she answered. "I am tired and hungry and will stay here for the night."

The guards discussed it between them, and then nodded.

"As you wish, my lady." They helped her from the horse, and she hated every moment of it. Then they escorted her to the door of the inn. As she entered, she looked over her shoulder one last time, but figured it was the last she'd seen of the man named Madoc.

The guards accompanied her to a table that cleared of its occupants as soon as she approached. In a matter of seconds, the innkeeper was at her side with a plate of food and a mug of ale in his hands.

"Would there be anything else for you, my lady?" he asked, bowing so low she wanted to kick him in the chin.

"Nay," she answered, then changed her mind. "Aye. I'd like a hot bath prepared in a private room of my own with a minstrel sent up to play the lute and spout poetry while I sip my wine."

"Aye, my lady, I'll see to it at once." The innkeeper bowed three more times before rushing over to his wife. They discussed her request in hushed words and then hurried around to attend to her needs.

"The fools," she muttered under her breath. She was only being sarcastic, yet they jumped at her every word.

"'Twould be wise to go above stairs as soon as they prepare your chamber," Desmond told her. "The tavern inside here attracts ruffians and 'tis not proper to loiter among the ragpickers."

"I will finish my food and ale, and retire as I see fit." Once again, they told her what to do. But she wasn't in the castle now and they would abide by her decisions this time.

Abigail watched the fools hauling a wooden tub up the stairs, nearly falling backwards as it slipped and started to roll. Then the serving wenches followed, climbing the stairs next, as they carefully took hot buckets of water, one by one, to fill it. Wouldn't they be surprised when she decided she didn't want it after all? Tiring of hearing the guards' idle chatter, she decided being locked in a room by herself was a good start to planning her next escape.

"I do not want to be bothered all night once I go to my chamber," she instructed the guards.

"Aye, my lady. We will stand watch at the door to protect you." Emric supplied the information she didn't want to hear.

"Nay," she answered quickly. "That is not necessary."

"Your father would have it no other way." Desmond helped her to her feet and guided her up the old, wooden staircase.

Her father shouldn't care, as he was the one who decided to send her away to her doom. As she ascended the stairs, she looked over her shoulder once more to the open room below. Scanning the patrons, she did not see Madoc amongst them. With a sigh, she turned around and entered her room.

"I shall attend to your bath," said a young girl in the room who she guessed to be the innkeeper's daughter.

Abigail needed to think and didn't want anyone waiting on her tonight. She just wanted to be left alone.

"I will attend to myself," she told the girl. The girl nodded and left. As Abigail closed the door, she saw the guards handing her a coin.

Abigail rested her head against the closed door, tired and weary. On the morrow, she would be delivered to Lord Shrewsbury and soon after that, she would be the ogre's wife. Why had she thought her life could be different? For some reason, she really believed the man named Madoc would care for her and take her away from her problems.

She spied an old, wooden cup with wine sitting on a small night table. It was next to a worn sleeping pallet that had no dais but was thrown right down upon the rushes. The pallet was probably flea-ridden but she really didn't care. She was so tired from her travels she figured even the biting of bugs wouldn't rouse her.

As she removed her clothing, her gaze fell upon the steaming barrel of water that would serve as her bath. "It would feel good on my aching muscles," she decided. She had just removed her clothing and slipped beneath the water when there was a knock at the door.

"The minstrel is here, my lady, at your request," came the guard's voice. "Shall I send him inside, or would you require me to accompany him?"

"Send him away," she called out, sinking lower into the steamy water, basking in the glory of the small tub.

"I am here to sing and spout poetry to your little heart's desire," came the voice of the minstrel from the other side of door.

Her eyes popped open. She knew that voice and mocking tone. It was the thief come back to taunt her!

"Send him in alone and leave us be," she called out.

The door creaked open and then slammed shut again. In the dim light of the night candle, she saw a man in colorful clothing with a ridicules hat upon his head. The hat spouted two long, raggedy plumes off to one side that looked as if they'd just been plucked from a goose in the midst of a struggle. In his hand, he carried not a lute but a gemshorn – hollowed out animal horn – sometimes played like a flute.

She couldn't see his face well in the shadows, but this man had no beard, nor a mustache. He was not her thief.

"Oh!" she exclaimed. "Go away, go away!" She sank deeper into the water, crossing her arms over her chest.

"Make up your mind," he growled, heading toward the

door. "And stop begging me to let you tag along if you don't mean it."

"Madoc?" She sat up taller in the tub, trying to see his face in the dark.

"Well, did you think these peasants really had a minstrel on hand for your beck and call?"

She squinted, trying to see his face. "Come closer."

When he stepped into the candlelight, she could tell it was, indeed, her thief. His freshly-shaven face looked strong and handsome. He had a long, straight nose and a small cleft in his chin. His mouth was pursed, but his lips looked soft – just right for kissing. And his eyes were most alluring. They glimmered like clear, green emeralds in the candlelight.

"I'll play the horn and spout poetry, but don't expect me to scrub your back. If I get any closer to you, I won't be responsible for my actions. You do realize, I haven't had a woman in quite some time now."

She sank back into the water, having almost forgotten she was sitting in a room totally naked with a rogue. What was she thinking? And what were her addlepated guards thinking to actually grant her this outrageous request of letting him in the room?

There was another knock at the door, and then the sound of Desmond's voice. "Are you faring well, my lady? I hear no music from within."

Her head whipped around toward the door, and her heart raced. She didn't want the guard coming in, nor did she want Madoc to leave.

"Play music," she whispered to him. "Quickly!"

He rolled his eyes and shook his head, then settled himself on the old worn mattress and raised the horn to his mouth.

He blew a sour note, and then another. It made her want to cover her ears.

"You call that music?" she gasped.

"Well, forgive me your nobleness, but it was all I could do to scrape up these silly clothes on such short notice. No one around here carries a lute on their back, and this was the only instrument I could find."

"Where did you get those things?"

He threw the horn down on the pallet, running his tongue over his teeth as if he didn't like the taste of it. "Don't worry about it, sweetie." He then took it upon himself to pick up the cup and guzzle down the wine.

Once more came a knock at the door, and the guard's voice was heard again. "I don't hear music, my lady. Is everything all right?"

She looked over to Madoc urgently, but he slowly shook his head. It was apparent he wasn't going to play the horn again. Actually, in a way, she was glad.

"He is spouting poetry," she called out to the guard. "And very admirable, I must admit." She turned to look at him and raised her eyebrows. "Well?"

"Well, what?" he asked, pulling a loaf of bread out of his clothing that she was sure he lifted somewhere along the way.

"Spout poetry," she commanded. "If not, the guards will come in and haul you away."

"You have got to be jesting," he said in a low, deep voice. But when another knock came at the door, he jumped to his feet.

"My lady of deceit . . . you have nice . . . feet . . ." he started, scratching his head in the process.

"Make it sound real," she snapped.

"I have no clue what poets say. I live in the woods by myself, remember?"

"Surely you've heard poets in the castle when you saw to – help yourself to what you wanted?"

His nostrils flared at those words and he crossed his arms over his chest. "Too bad I don't see anything I want right now," he said, looking directly at her.

She sank deeper into the water, not liking his insinuation. "Just try," she begged him. "Please."

MADOC HAD every intention of leaving her stranded, but when Abigail begged him with her innocent blue eyes he couldn't resist. She may have an air about her of being superior but, after all, she had been raised in luxury and pampered all her life. Mayhap, he shouldn't hold that against her.

He walked closer and when he neared her, he could see through the water to her naked body. She tried to hide from him, but the tub was small and therefore left little to his imagination. His eyes traveled down her soft, rounded shoulders to her arms crossed in front of her breasts. He noticed the swells beneath, and the rosy tip of one nipple peeking out. Her stomach was taut. And though her legs were pushed together, he could still see the silken, golden curls at the juncture of her thighs.

His manhood hardened and he closed his eyes, trying to push away the lust inside that made him want to take her right now. She was correct – he always took whatever he wanted. But this was different. She was a lady. Even though she was naked, he wouldn't take from her what she wasn't willing to give. After all, even a thief had his scruples.

He opened his eyes, walking closer to her, kneeling down by the side of the tub.

"My Lady, you are the fresh mountain breeze that dances on the vale. Your hair is golden threads of the gods spun with . . . sunbeams. Your eyes are a midsummer's night . . . cool, alluring. And your skin is as soft as the clouds that span the heavens and also cover a man's aching heart."

"That was beautiful," she said in a sultry whisper. "Please . . . more," she urged him to continue.

He'd been speaking from his heart, but when she straightened in the tub and unknowingly gave him full view of both glorious breasts, his lust overtook him once again.

"The swells of your mountains make a man want to bury his head between them and plant his seed within the juncture of your golden fields."

"What?" she said with a gasp as her mouth turned down in a frown.

"The slapping sea, thrusting forcefully against the cliffs, willing the cave to open . . ."

"Stop!" she cried, grabbing the drying cloth from the edge of the tub. Giving him one last peek of her nakedness, she rose up and wrapped the cloth around her. "Get out," she said softly, then, "get out!" much louder. Her eyes closed and her body trembled.

"Did I do something to displease you, my lady?" Madoc wasn't even aware of what he'd said. "I was spouting poetry as you requested."

"Well, stop it, at once," she ordered. "And stop calling me, *my lady*. My name is Abigail."

There was one last knock at the door and, this time, the

guard poked his head inside. "I heard you cry out, my lady. Shall I remove the minstrel?"

Madoc's eyes interlocked with hers. Indeed, she had cried out. And if he stayed there any longer he'd have her crying out for an entirely different reason.

"No need," Madoc replied before she could answer. "I can see myself out." With a slight nod of his head, he bid her goodbye and headed out the door.

"Shall I have the tub removed, my lady?" asked the guard.

"Nay," she answered. "And I do not want to be disturbed again this night."

"As you wish," he said and closed the door.

Abigail's body quivered beneath the drying cloth but it wasn't from the cold. Her loins burned beneath it, and it was all Madoc's fault. He had enraptured her with his poetry by praising her beauty. But when he'd started comparing other things, she knew the lust he held for her inside. And she couldn't deny the fact she was feeling the same thing.

This scared her and excited her at the same time. As she stepped from the tub, she let the drying cloth drop to the ground. Burning heat warmed the area between her thighs and she realized her nipples had hardened.

She clasped her hand over her mouth and tears formed in her eyes. Would she feel this way when she was married to the Lord of Shrewsbury? Most likely not. Madoc stirred things inside her that she didn't know how to control. And now, to her dismay, she'd dismissed him from her life. Because of her action, she would die with the burning passion inside, as she would never see the thief who'd stolen her heart again.

CHAPTER 5

*A*bigail shifted on the pallet. A splashing noise in the room woke her from her slumber. She'd been so tired that she'd slept throughout the night without even waking. Her window was open to cleanse the musty smell of the room, and the birds twittered outside cheerfully. The sun streamed in through the opening as it rose higher on the horizon.

"Did you sleep well, my lady – I mean Abbey?"

Pushing up to a sitting position, she rubbed her eyes and tried to clear her head. She couldn't have just heard Madoc's voice, could she? Hearing more splashing, her attention went to the tub. Sure enough, there sat Madoc, knees bent and almost touching his chin since his large body was smashed into the small tub of cold water.

"How did you get in here?" she asked curiously, knowing she had locked the door.

He scrubbed his hair with the soft soap that was in a bowl at the side of the tub. "You really shouldn't sleep with your window open. You don't know who is going to drop in." He bent over and dunked his head in the water and came up with a sharp intake of breath. "God's teeth, that's cold!" When he stood, she quickly redirected her gaze so he wouldn't catch her looking at him.

Rising from the pallet, Abigail headed over to look out the second story window. "This is high," she said, stretching her neck to see the ground far below. "How did you get up here without falling?"

He dried off with the cloth as he answered. "That was easy compared to finding the proper attire for our travels."

"*Our* travels?" Her head snapped around in surprise to hear this. When she did, she found herself looking directly at his naked body as he used the towel to dry his hair. Her eyes curiously traveled downward and settled on his nether region. A gasp left her mouth when she saw his manhood ramrod straight. Her eyes shot back up to his face. His cocky grin told her he was enjoying every second of this. "Mayhap, the water wasn't quite as cold as you thought after all, was it?" she asked.

"I am pleased that you noticed." He pulled on the clothes he'd obviously pilfered, because they were the clothes of one of her guards. Then he threw a bundle and it landed on the bed. "Put those on," he told her.

She walked over to inspect the contents of the package. It was a peasant's attire. And by the looks of it, it had been used.

"I don't wear soiled clothing, but thank you." She held the things out by the tips of her fingers, waiting for him to take them. But he did nothing of the sort.

"They're not soiled," he said, running his fingers through his wet hair to try to straighten it. "The wench didn't have them on long enough to get them dirty."

"So . . . you bedded a serving wench to get her clothes?"

She turned to look at him and he had that damned grin on his face again.

"Would it bother you if I had?"

It bothered her immensely but she wouldn't let him know it. She also wasn't in a hurry to have him find out how she had longed for him after he left her last night.

"Nay," she said with a sniff. "It doesn't matter to me in the least. Now, look away while I change."

He chuckled at that. "You didn't seem to have any qualms about me looking at your naked body last night."

"Well, that won't happen again."

"Don't be so sure."

She turned away from him and donned the clothes. Her proportions were a bit larger than the woman who'd worn these clothes. Abigail's breasts were trussed up and overexposed. She yanked at the laces to draw them together.

"You must like your women small. These clothes don't fit me at all."

"Let's see." Madoc walked over to her and put his hands on her shoulders. He turned her around and she looked up to meet his eyes. However, he was looking down her bodice instead of at her face. "Nay, you are wrong," he mumbled. "The clothes fit perfectly." With that he gave the ties on her bodice a playful yank and the lacing popped open, exposing her even more.

"I am not one of your playthings," she retorted, putting everything back in place. "You would be wise to remember I am not a wench you can tumble in the night and think naught of it. Just like you did to the girl who owned these clothes," she added as an afterthought.

She tried to step away, but his hand on her shoulder stopped him.

"For your information, I did not bed the wench, but took her clothes as she partnered with another patron."

"Oh." Abigail looked up into his gorgeous, green eyes and wished she hadn't. He was staring down at her lips. "Why did you come back when I told you to leave?" she asked, her voice coming out as naught more than a muffled whisper. She couldn't even think when she was so close to him like this. He smelled fresh and clean. And though his skin was cool from the water, she felt the warmth of his hand upon her skin.

"I wasn't going to," he admitted. "But I couldn't ignore the wanting you held for me in your eyes last night. I just couldn't deprive you of that, Abbey."

His lips brushed against hers in a whisper of a kiss. Her eyes closed of their own accord and her head fell back. When he brought his mouth back to hers a second time, she parted her lips slightly, welcoming the kiss and wanting more. He might not have had a woman in a while but he was experienced, that she could tell. With the way he kissed her, she found herself wanting to do so much more. He nibbled her lips softly, pulling her closer with both hands up against his hard chest.

"I don't want you," she lied. "And my name is Abigail, not Abbey."

He kissed her again, this time letting his hands roam, sliding them around the back of her to rest on her bottom.

"You are just as bad a liar as me," he said against her lips, giving her bottom a playful squeeze.

She felt that same warming between her thighs that he'd triggered last night. As she held her breath, her legs became weak beneath her. Next, his kisses trailed down her neck, stopping just above her collarbone.

"I like calling you Abbey," he continued. "It suits you, since you remind me of an innocent girl from a nunnery." His mouth traveled to her cleavage and she couldn't help but let out another gasp of surprise. His tongue shot out and traced the crease between her trussed up breasts.

Her fingers tightened as she grabbed on to his hair. Then she surprised herself when she pulled his head closer. Letting out a small moan, vibrations from her womanhood felt arousing as they were awoken from his teasing. Then, when he thought to slip his hand inside her chemise to fondle her breast, she knew she had to stop him or they would end up naked upon the pallet within a matter of minutes. With all her might and against her will, she pushed out of his embrace and stepped away from him.

"I've never had a rogue before," she admitted. She'd never had anyone before except for the few kisses shared between her and the stable boy but she wasn't going to tell him that.

"But it excites you to think about it doesn't it?" He gently pulled her back into his arms, the action causing her body to quiver. He was right. The thought of making love to him excited her, indeed. Everything about Madoc ap Powell had her senses reeling. The way he looked at her and the way he spoke made her heart beat faster. It even excited her every time he came up with a new disguise. She was also fascinated by his skill of being a birdman. Right now, she wanted him so badly she'd almost forgotten she was on her way to marry someone else, until they were interrupted by a rapping noise on the door.

"My lady, please ready yourself as we need to leave for Shrewsbury Castle anon."

"The guards!" she said. Instantly, their intimate embrace was broken. "Can you get us out of here without them knowing?" she whispered.

"We can go out the way I came in," he said, putting on the cloak and fastening her dagger at his side.

Abigail looked over to the high window in horror and then back at him. "I can't. I'm afraid."

"Afraid?" He tightened his belt as he spoke. "I didn't figure you would be afraid of anything, my lady. Except for marrying the Lord of Shrewsbury." He mumbled the last part.

Madoc pushed the peasant's shoes into her hand while he settled the drab brown cape around her shoulders. It was so unlike her royal purple one that she loved, but she knew she'd be spotted too easily if she wore it.

"I don't like heights," she admitted. "I fell out of a tree as a child and have been terrified of heights ever since."

"Unbelievable," she heard him growl, pacing back and forth, obviously trying to come up with a new plan. "You do realize that if I am caught, I will end up in a dungeon again. And let me tell you, I have a strong aversion to dungeons."

"*Again?*" she asked, but he ignored her.

Instead, he picked up her noble gown and shoved it into her hands. "Hand this out the door to the guard but don't let him see you. Tell him you've spilled wine on it and need it cleaned before you can travel. Tell him to take the gown to the innkeeper's wife."

"What?" she asked as he guided her to the door with his hand at the small of her back.

"Just do it – and quickly," he said in a hushed whisper. He

picked up her purple cloak in the process.

She did as she was told and handed the gown to the guard. Madoc stopped her from closing the door, and peered out until he was sure the man had gone down to the kitchen. Then he threw the purple cloak over her shoulders, right over the brown cape.

"Now hurry," he told her. "And don't talk to anyone along the way." He pushed her out in front of him, and he followed along in his guardsman's disguise. They made it all the way down the stairs and were heading for the front door when the innkeeper approached them.

"I thought you needed your gown cleaned, my lady," said the man.

Madoc stopped her from turning around and, instead, talked to the man over his shoulder. "She decided it was fine after all," he said in a deep, authoritative voice, trying to sound like a castle guard. He then rushed her through the door to the awaiting horses.

"Where are my clothes?" A guard called from inside the building.

Madoc rushed her to his horse and lifted her into the saddle. He followed suit, pulling himself up behind her.

"Shouldn't we take a second horse?" she asked, looking around to try to find one.

"No time," he said. "They'll be on our tails in a second. Plus, I can't risk that you might ride off on me, and put us both in danger again. This time, I'm in charge."

With that, he kicked his heels into the horse and they sped away before they were discovered. They rode hard and off the beaten path for a while before he even thought to slow down.

Abigail felt the blood push through her veins at all the

excitement. Her life had been far from boring ever since she'd met Madoc. He was naught but a scoundrel and a thief. But the oddest part was that she felt safe in his arms. His body pressed up against hers and she rocked in his embrace with every step of the horse. Thoughts – crazy thoughts filled her head that she'd almost made love to him and that she wouldn't have regretted it in the least. Abigail felt alive for the first time in her life! This mysterious thief and everything about him was wrong. But she wouldn't trade it for all the gold in her father's coffers.

Madoc was danger and excitement all rolled into one. He was as dishonest as the day was long and should be locked up forever for the things he'd done, but she liked it. She liked it so much it scared her to wonder who she really was. Sadly, she no longer knew. All she knew was that when she was with Madoc, she never wanted to be anywhere else.

"So, where are we off to now on our next adventure?" she asked with a smile on her face.

"No more detours or things to slow me down," he answered. "And we're not getting off this horse again until we get to Shrewsbury."

The blood pumped hard through her veins again but, this time, it was for a very different reason.

"Please, anywhere but Shrewsbury," she begged, knowing it wasn't going to make a difference. He had made up his mind and try as hard as she could, she wasn't going to be able to change it.

He didn't even respond to her plea.

Suddenly, their travels were less exciting and the smile disappeared from her face. Shrewsbury was the last place in the world that she wanted to be right now.

CHAPTER 6

*T*was just about nightfall when they rode into the town of Shrewsbury. Madoc could see the castle in the distance and also feel Abbey's body tense in his arms when she noticed it, too. Still, he didn't have a choice. Here is where his mother lived and he felt like he'd already wasted too much time in getting here.

He'd only stopped once on the trip to let Abbey use a bush. That's when he changed out of the guard's clothes and donned his own in order not to cause suspicion. He'd also made Abbey hide her purple cloak.

Madoc could see the tall wall surrounding their town. It was much like the castle, surrounded by an outer wall, with towers on each side of the entrance. The town's gates were about to be closed so he picked up the pace and, thankfully, managed to get there just in time.

"Madoc, 'tis been a while," said Barclay, the man at the gate, nodding to him as he rode through.

"Aye," he mumbled to acknowledge him, but kept on riding. He would have rather not had anyone see him since he was a fugitive. He usually kept out of sight. But he couldn't sneak in tonight through the hole in the town's crumbling wall as he usually did. Not with Abbey and the horse along. Many of the town's people liked him so he knew he'd have their loyalty to keep his whereabouts a secret. However, he wasn't so sure about Barclay. While the man guarded the gate, he sincerely doubted Barclay could guard his secret.

ABBEY WAS THRILLED to get her first look at an actual town. She'd never been allowed anywhere but in her castle's demesne while living with her father. When her mother was alive, she had tried to convince her father to let her explore, but was unable to sway him to do so.

"So, this is the town," she remarked. She tried to look around, but it was dark and the street was not lit.

"Don't get your hopes up. 'Tis nothing compared to living in a castle."

A pig squealed and ran out in front of them, scaring her for a moment. She jerked backward and felt Madoc's arm tighten around her protectively. "What's that?"

"'Tis called a sow," he remarked in a low voice, his breath tickling her hair since his mouth was right next to her ear. "I would have thought you had those at your castle."

"It startled me, that is all," she said stiffly, not amused at his subtle way of calling her ignorant. "And, of course, I can iden-tify a sow."

She noticed a foul smell in the streets and heard a voice mumble from up above her head. Instantly, Madoc yanked the reins and, thankfully, just in time to avoid being hit by someone dumping a bucket from the second floor window into the street. The contents splashed up and a few droplets hit her cape.

"What was that?" she asked in astonishment.

"You won't find garderobes here, sweetie, so get used to it."

She suddenly realized they were dumping their sewage into the street. Her stomach soured and she wanted to rip the cape from her body in disgust.

"Where are all the people?" she asked, noticing the nearly empty cobblestoned streets.

"'Tis late," he explained. "Curfew is in force, and no one is allowed out at night because 'tis not safe. If they do go out after dark for any reason, they are to have a lantern. If not, they will be mistaken for a ruffian."

"Well, I suppose you would know all about that," she replied snidely.

Curfew? Abbey pondered the thought. It sounded a lot like life in the castle with gates to lock her in, and someone telling her not to go into the streets at night. This truly surprised her.

Just then a loud bell clanged from atop the tower. The remaining few people on the street disappeared indoors and Madoc picked up the pace.

"Is that the curfew bell?" she asked, trying to jest. But when he grunted and nodded his head, she realized he'd really meant it.

"The bells will ring to announce everything," he explained. "The next will be to signal the opening of the market at first light on the morrow."

Madoc stopped in front of a house that had two levels, as were most of the establishments. The structures were wooden and some of them whitewashed as well. It looked to her like merchants' shops were on the bottom dark floors. By the candles burning in the windows above, she figured the second stories must be where the residents lived.

"This is where we get off, Abbey." Madoc dismounted quickly and held out his arms to help her from the horse. She allowed him to do it, liking the way it felt as he grabbed her so close to her breasts it made her inhale sharply. She dismounted, sliding down his body slowly until her feet hit the ground. He paused when their bodies touched each other. Then he released a frustrated breath.

"Is this where your mother lives?" she asked as he tied up his horse to a post out front. He grunted instead of replying, making her wonder if something was bothering him.

He climbed the stairs on the side of the structure leading to the upper floor. She hesitated a moment and then cautiously followed. When she got halfway up the narrow, rickety staircase, she made the mistake of looking down. Her head dizzied and she had to grab on to the railing with two hands and stop. She didn't like the height and was afraid of falling to the ground far below.

"Don't tell me you are afraid?" he asked, looking over his shoulder and stopping when he realized she no longer followed. He came back down to meet her, grabbing her hand in the process. "Let's go, precious."

He pulled her up behind him and through a door into the house above.

"Madoc!" A man sitting at a table with a needle and thread in hand looked up from his work. Then he threw the items down on the table, jumped up and joined them.

"William." Madoc embraced the man quickly. "How is mother? I got Homer's message. What's wrong?"

"She has taken a turn for the worse," he told Madoc with a

solemn look upon his face. "Nothing I do seems to help her." Then the man turned his attention to Abigail. "Who is she, Madoc? Did you marry while you were away?"

Abbey felt her face flush at the suggestion and she dropped her gaze to the rough, wooden floor. There was a fire burning in the hearth, helping to take the chill from the air. This building was not the finest, but was certainly much nicer than the hut Madoc had built.

"That's . . . Abbey," he told William. "I found her in a tavern. Abbey, this is my brother, William."

She was aghast by his proclamation of finding her in a tavern, but William didn't seem to care. She nodded a quick greeting to Madoc's brother. Then, instead of giving her any more attention, the men continued talking.

"What is wrong with Mother? Is she dying? The message sounded urgent," said Madoc.

"We don't know, and are afraid to call in anyone to heal her. After the barber bled her last week, she took a turn for the worse. We don't want them to say 'tis the plague and cast us out."

Abbey wondered if anyone besides William and his mother lived there.

"I understand," said Madoc. "But is it the plague? I thought after taking almost half the town we were free from it by now."

"I don't believe that is what ails her. The plague hasn't been seen here for some time now, and she hasn't got the symptoms. But come; she will be happy to see you."

They disappeared into an adjoining room, leaving Abbey standing there by herself. Never in all her years at the castle had anyone ignored her or not seen to her needs before their own.

She decided she kind of liked it in a way, not having all the attention focused on her. Strolling over to the fire, Abbey warmed her hands while taking in her surroundings.

'Twas a small room she occupied, with a wooden table and benches in the center. There were two doors leading to other rooms that she guessed were the bedchambers. Two large chests were pushed along the far wall, and shelves that held bolts of material used for making clothing were above them. There was a tall cupboard in one corner, and a basket on the floor full of wooden spools wound with colored threads. Some boxes were stacked against the wall, threatening to tip over in a wobbly-looking pile.

Spying a garment lying on top of the table, she strolled over to inspect it. So William was a tailor. And by the looks of the beautiful gown he'd been working on, he was very good at his craft. She ran her hand over the bright reddish-orange silk skirt attached to a matching velvet bodice, marveling at the small, precise stitching used on the piece.

This was a very expensive fabric and a color that had only recently been seen worn by the nobles. Commoners were only supposed to wear brown, black, or other drab clothes made from coarse material like wool, burlap or even canvas. She wondered as to why he would even be crafting such a piece? What was it doing here? If someone from the castle had summoned him to make it, surely he would be paid well for this garment.

Madoc appeared in the doorway looking as if he'd just discovered she wasn't with him. Or perhaps, he was just checking to make certain she hadn't slipped away.

"Abbey, come here," he called. "I want you to meet my mother."

She hesitated, having heard talk of the plague.

He motioned with his hand for her to come forward. "I have seen plenty of the plague and she hasn't got it," he reassured her. "Now, come. Please." He still had his hand out, waiting for her to accept it. Her heart fluttered by the fact he'd said please. There was no way she could deny his request when she saw a soft, caring look in his eyes. She walked forward and put her hand in his. Together, they continued into the room and over to join William and the woman in a raised bed.

"Mother, this is Abbey." Madoc gave no further introduction, nor did he need to. The elderly woman pushed up to the sitting position and perused her.

"You brought a lady of the castle here? Are you mad?" she asked in a shaky voice.

Abbey was shocked that the woman could see through her disguise so easily. She didn't know what to say.

"She's not staying," Madoc told his mother, surprising her even more. "She just needs a place to . . . spend the night."

"You are running from someone, aren't you?" the woman asked, looking directly at her.

Abbey's eyes shot over to Madoc for support, but he was looking at the floor. She then looked at William, but he seemed very nervous as well.

"You shouldn't have brought her here," William whispered to Madoc. Still, Abbey heard him. "You have put us all in danger."

"Aye," agreed his mother. "And with William about to appeal to the guild for approval, this jeopardizes everything he has worked so hard for. He's spent the last seven years preparing."

"I – I am sorry," she sputtered, feeling like such a burden. "I will leave, then." She turned abruptly with tears in her eyes. Before she took two steps, Madoc reached out and stopped her.

"She is here by my request, Mother," he told the woman. "I assure you, she will do naught to jeopardize William's appeal to the guild, nor put any of us in danger. I give you my word."

Abbey felt relieved that Madoc came to her defense, but she knew they were right and she should not be there. She didn't want to endanger anyone, but she had nowhere else to go.

"Mother needs her rest," said William, all but pushing them back out into the main room. He closed the door behind them. "Have you eaten?" he asked, motioning with his hand toward the table. He collected his work, moving the gown from the table to make room for them to sit. "I have a thick pottage on the fire," he told them, placing bowls down in front of them.

"I have to tend to my birds," Madoc said instead of answering. He walked away abruptly and went out a back door. Abbey saw him climb the stairs to yet another level, leaving her there alone with William.

"So, who are you really?" asked William, spooning food into a bowl in front of her. "Madoc keeps to himself and has never brought a woman home – and certainly not a lady."

Her stomach growled when she eyed the food. It looked delicious. A hearty aroma filled the air from the thick pottage that looked like it included cabbage, carrots and leeks. She settled herself upon the bench, picked up the spoon, and started eating. The warm food was a good contrast from the chill of the night air.

"I am Lady Abigail of Blackmore," she said, balancing her next spoonful of food precariously in front of her. "I was being sent to marry the Lord of Shrewsbury when your brother decided to rob us."

"He is not my brother," explained William, dishing out food for him and sitting across from her. "Not really. Although we were raised as brothers, I am quite a bit older than Madoc."

"Then what is he to you?"

William looked at her as he spoke. "I was an orphan taken in by our mother at a young age. I was . . . here . . . when Madoc was . . . born."

Something bothered this man immensely. He was just as bad a liar as Madoc. There was something this family was hiding and she made it her challenge to find out what.

"So, where is Madoc's father? Does he live here, too?" She took another bite, delighting in the simplicity of the meal. It was so unlike the stuffed pheasant or eel eggs she was used to eating. This was the food of the poor, but she really liked it.

"Nay. He is –"

"Dead! His father is dead." Madoc's mother stood in the entranceway of her room, holding on to the door for support. Her eyes looked sunken on her ashen face, and she stood bent over. Within her eyes, Abbey witnessed an angry, intense fire.

"Mother," said William, jumping up to help her. "Let me help you get back to bed." He wrapped a supporting arm around her, and they disappeared into her bedchamber.

Just then Madoc returned, looking curious as usual. His

eyes bore into her. "What were you telling them?" he asked, first looking toward the bedroom and then back to her.

Abbey continued eating her food. "'Tis not what I was telling them, but what they were telling me."

He looked to her with a questioning brow and helped himself to a heaping bowl of the pottage. Then he settled across from her in the spot William had vacated.

"And what would that be?"

"That William isn't really your brother, and your father isn't really dead." She didn't look up because she didn't want to see his expression.

"They told you that?" His voice was deep and stern.

"Only the first half. But they didn't need to say more. I figured out the rest on my own. They are poor liars, the same as you."

"Well, don't be asking about my family again. And don't tell them anything about yours," he said as an afterthought.

"Too late for that," she said with a smile.

He shook his head and ran a weary hand through his hair. Just then, William came out and joined them, closing the door behind him.

"Mother is very upset for some reason. But I think she will sleep now," William relayed the information. "I will stay with her tonight and you two can share my room."

Abigail's head snapped up at that, and her eyes opened wide. It was apparent William had thought they had already coupled and that they would be doing it again tonight.

"Nay. I will sleep out here by the fire," she said.

William exchanged glances with Madoc.

"Nay," said Madoc, looking directly at her. "I will stay out here instead, and you will take the sleeping pallet."

She didn't argue with him, but excused herself and went into the room and closed the door.

ONCE SHE WAS GONE, William joined Madoc at the table. "You put us in grave danger bringing her here. Mother is very upset."

"I realize that," stated Madoc. "But I had no choice. They were going to take her to marry Lord Shrewsbury and she doesn't want to go."

"So, because of it, you saw to make that decision for her by helping hide her from the nobility?"

"Since when have I ever made a decision that you or Mother agreed with? And by the way, I don't like that you were telling her about our family. I have always considered you my true brother. Although you were once an orphan, you didn't have to tell her that. And why in Heaven's name does she think my father is still alive? She thinks you and Mother are lying. Are you?"

William didn't answer but, in his eyes, Madoc could see 'twas true.

"Who is my father, William? Why don't you tell me?"

"I made a promise to your mother years ago. Because of all she's done for me, I cannot break it."

Madoc finished off his dinner and helped himself to Abbey's leftovers. William handed him a mug of ale that he proceeded to chug down in aggravation.

"I always felt something wasn't right, yet I could never get a straight answer from either of you," growled Madoc. "Now, tell me what it is you are keeping from me, William."

William looked down and shook his head as if this secret

were eating him up from the inside out. "Ask your mother," was all he said. "Or mayhap Abbey, as she is very observant and seems to know more than you give her credit for."

"I'll do that," said Madoc, laying back on the bench and covering his face with his arm. He drifted off to sleep knowing the morrow was going to be one hell of a day.

CHAPTER 7

*A*bbey awoke hearing the sound of a clanging bell drifting in through the open bedroom window. She guessed it was signaling the opening of the market at first light, as Madoc had mentioned last night. She opened one sleepy eye, and then closed it again, not ready to start her day. She'd slept in the nude, not wanting to wear the soiled wench's clothes nor the cape that was splattered with things she'd yet to decipher.

She pulled the coverlet higher and rolled to her other side. She gasped when she realized Madoc was lying next to her. He was atop the covers and as naked as she.

"Good morning, sunshine." He had his eyes closed and lay on his back.

"What are you doing here?" She gripped the bedcovers tightly, holding them up to her chin.

"Sleeping, same as you."

"I thought you were sleeping in the other room."

"After the third time falling off the bench I felt this would be the safer of the choices."

He turned to look at her then and his eyes drank her in. This was not the safer of the choices and he certainly knew it. He also knew she was naked beneath the coverlet. She was certain of this because of what she saw below his waist. She gasped again and turned away.

"Cover up," she told him. "Have a little respect for a lady." In one swift motion, he joined her under the covers. "That's not what I meant." She turned to face him.

"But that is what you said." He reached out and traced her lips with his finger.

Her tongue darted out to moisten her lips and that motion seemed to drive him from his mind. He leaned over then and placed his mouth against hers. She liked the way it felt and let him. And she also did naught to stop him when he cradled her head with his hand and deepened the kiss, letting his tongue slip into her mouth.

It felt so wonderful that she couldn't bring herself to push him away. Something about this man's kisses made her forget all her troubles and feel safe instead. Safe that she was with a man who could protect her and help her. Safe that she was with . . . a thief? What in the name of St. Blaise was she doing?

He kissed her again, this time, his mouth closing around her bottom lip and pulling lightly in a tease. Then he kissed her gently atop her nose. His methods of seduction were drawing her in, and she could no longer tell herself that this is not what she really wanted.

She welcomed him as he slipped his tongue into her mouth again, and matched him with her own this time. It was exciting to feel wicked as she lay naked under the covers with a man she barely knew. Her heart beat furiously. She liked it, she decided, pushing the thoughts from her head that this was not the expected behavior of a lady. Then she pushed more thoughts from her head of what her father would say or do to her if he knew what she was even considering doing right now.

Madoc stroked her hair in a tender caress. The heat from his body engulfed her. She felt that warming vibration between her legs and knew if she started something, this time, they would not be able to stop.

She didn't care, she realized. Abbey had lived by everyone else's choices her entire life. It was time she start living by her own choices now, even if it was unheard of and frowned upon for a woman to act in this manner. After all, her father thought naught of her own feelings or needs when he decided to trade her away like yesterday's stale bread as Lord Shrewsbury's bride. He was using her as a pawn to secure the release of her brother. When would she ever have the chance to do anything of her choosing again? Once she was married to the Lord of Shrewsbury, her life would be over. In her heart, she wished she could experience surrendering to her passions and know what it felt like to make love with a man who excited her in ways she could never even imagine.

"You want this as much as I do, don't you?" he whispered, slipping his hand under the covers to gently fondle her breast.

She jumped at the feel of the coolness of his fingers, but warmed instantly when he continued to caress her. His fingers played with her nipple, causing it to go taut. A surge of heat ran its course through her, and she boldly reached out and touched him in the same manner.

He inhaled sharply and closed his eyes. Then he grew beneath her touch.

"I do," she answered wickedly and loved every minute of it.

She felt so alive and her body pulsated in anticipation of his length.

"You won't stop me this time?" he asked, letting his hand roam lower, exploring the juncture between her thighs. She moaned and opened her legs for him, allowing his finger to slip inside.

"I want you," she admitted. "I want you more than anything." His fingers played with her and she felt her liquid passion guiding his fingers as he slipped in and out. She moaned slightly and opened wider. Her body pulsated against his hand.

"And you won't regret this later?"

"Nay," she said, unable to think anymore with a bit of reason. She could do naught to stop this now, even if she had wanted to. She pulled him closer, knowing he teased her to get the answer he wanted, but no longer caring. Abbey wanted him and needed him now more than anything in life. "Please . . . I can wait no longer."

That must have been what he was waiting to hear because, in one motion, he rolled atop her, using his arms to shield her from his weight. Then he looked at her once more, hesitating, and she wrapped her arms around his neck and her legs around his waist trying to urge him on. He slid inside her slowly then, as if he were waiting to see her reaction before he continued. His hardened manhood felt wonderful inside her and a moan of pleasure escaped her lips.

"Can you take in all of me?" he whispered in her ear, his tongue flicking her lobe in the process. Just the thought had her pulsating in readiness. She started to climax and couldn't respond. But her actions gave him the answer he needed.

He thrust his full length into her once. And when she

moved her hips to meet him, he continued thrusting again and again. That's when her world exploded in bright colors behind her closed lids. She needed him, wanted him – she wanted more. She arched and melded her body to his. They joined together, two lost souls now as one. And as they danced beneath the coverlet, her body met with his in passionate surrender.

Abbey couldn't help but think of Madoc's attempt at poetry and how he talked of the sea slapping against the cliffs and entering the cave. This thought only excited her more as she moved in rhythm beneath him. He was the sea and she the cliffs. Together, they joined as one. Her body felt hotter than fire burning against his in raging sensuous pleasure. She screamed out then, and he muffled her mouth with his, their kisses imitating their action under the covers.

And then he matched her excitement as he, too, was totally sated. He bit back a low, deep roar, his voice reverberating against her lips. Madoc let out the pent-up emotions she knew he'd been holding in since they'd met. Then he collapsed atop her, but being careful not to hurt her with his weight.

He rolled off of her to the side and pulled her atop him in the process. Abbey struggled to regain her breath and so did he. She had just done something vilely wicked. She could go to hell for her behavior. A smile pursed her lips since she was no longer afraid of the afterlife but focused on basking in the pleasures of her present life instead. Nay, she did not regret making love with Madoc, and she would do it again if she had the chance. Because this was something she'd been waiting for her entire life.

* * *

MADOC STOOD upon the roof later and opened the cage containing his birds. They seemed to be in good health. He had William to thank for that. William had been so busy with his trade and preparing his piece to present to the guild, that it had not been fair of Madoc to expect him to tend to the birds in his absence.

He watched the pigeons as they took off in flight. They circled around in the air and dropped back to the roof of the loft. They wouldn't go anywhere. They just needed exercise. They knew where home was, and always returned. He should let the flyers free that belonged back in Brynmawr. They needed to fly and to practice for the race. But first, he wanted to show them to Abbey.

Madoc often felt a lot like one of these birds. That's what attracted him to them in the first place. He had an aching in his heart to start a family and put down his roots in a real home – not in the upper floors of a wealthy tradesman's shop or an isolated hut in the mountains far away from civilization. But just like his two pens in two different places, he could not really call either of them home.

Family meant a lot to him, even if he only had his mother and William. Then he thought of Lord Corbett back at Blake Castle and how he'd found his long-lost sister, Wren. They seemed so happy, though they no longer had their parents. Each of them had made a home for themselves, be it England or Scotland, and each of them had also found a person to love. As siblings, they also had each other.

Madoc had never been in love before. He'd never allowed himself to fall for a woman because he didn't want to lose control. But now he wondered if he'd made a mistake because he was infatuated with a lady that he could never have.

"Madoc? Are you up there?"

He looked over the side railing and saw Abbey poking her head out the door below. She was wearing the new clothes he'd asked William to sew for her. She looked like a commoner now and would blend in well.

"Aye, come on up, my little bird."

She looked over at the ladder leading to the roof and shook her head. "Nay. I will wait for you here."

"Don't be afraid," he told her. "'Tis a beautiful view from up here. You can see the entire town."

When she shook her head again, he reached down a hand to help her.

"Nay, I can't," she said, seeming very shaken.

"Trust me, Abbey. 'Twill be all right."

She hesitated, but then looked up and her eyes met his. They had shared such intimate moments and it was something he would never forget. He only hoped she could drop her mistrust of him, even if he really was naught more than a thief in the night. Slowly, cautiously, her hand reached out to his and he directed it to the side of the wooden ladder.

"Now climb on up. 'Tis not hard."

"Is it safe?" she asked with a tremble in her voice. "I won't fall, will I?"

"Of course it is safe. You don't see the birds scared, do you? And I won't let you fall."

"I am not a bird," she pointed out, putting her foot on the rung. Then with a little coaxing from him, she made it to the top. He pulled her toward him and cradled her shaking body in his arms.

"Open your eyes," he said, when he realized she'd closed them tight in fear. "Look. You can see the whole town from up here."

ABBEY PUT her trust in Madoc, and was happy that she did. When she opened her eyes, she felt like a bird, looking down on the hustle and bustle of the streets below.

"'Tis amazing!" she cried, looking first to the peddlers on the streets and then to the children playing. She could hear the tradesmen calling out their wares, trying to pull customers into the open front areas of their shops. The streets were narrow and crowded, and life busied below her as people went about their daily business.

"You act as if you've never seen anything like this before."

"I haven't. My father didn't let me leave the castle walls, for fear he'd lose the last of his children."

"How so? What do you mean?" Madoc sat down with his back against the wooden building he'd built for his flock. Abbey sat in between his legs with her back toward him. He wrapped his arms around her, and it felt so right.

"I have two brothers," she explained. "But my brother, Edgar, I believe is dead. And I lost my mother to the plague not long ago."

"I'm sorry to hear that. But what do you mean you think he is dead? And what about your other brother?"

"Well, both my brothers, Edgar and Garrett, were sent overseas to fight for King Edward. When their ship was attacked by pirates, Edgar was captured, though Garrett was lucky enough to make it back alive.

"Garrett vowed he would find my brother, but after four

years of searching and also going back to battle, he came up with naught. And when he finally returned, my father was elated. But by then, Garrett had much anger locked inside him.

"One day, he tired of the feud between my father and the late Lord Shrewsbury. Against my father's will, he traveled to Shrewsbury, intending on killing the man in order to stop the feud. He was captured and thrown in the dungeon instead."

"So, the man you are to marry now holds your brother prisoner?"

"Aye. He is continuing what his father started. My brother has been in the dungeon of Shrewsbury Castle for nearly a year now. The late lord would have killed Garrett had he not fallen ill and died. His son, Lionel, saw an opportunity after his father's death, and therefore neither killed Garrett nor set him free. He is a greedy man. He knew he could get whatever he wanted from my father in a deal that involved the release of my brother."

"A dungeon is a horrible place to be," said Madoc shaking his head. "What was the feud about in the first place?"

"My father stole the late lord's betrothed. She ended up being my mother. I often wonder if the reason the man didn't kill my brother right away was because he still held a fondness for my mother after all these years and could not bear to kill her child. But now they are both gone and I am being punished in return. I am being sent as an offering. If I marry Lord Shrewsbury, he has agreed to set my brother free."

"Abbey, I didn't know." He placed a kiss atop her head. "I am so sorry."

"I no longer want to speak of my troubles. Tell me about your family, Madoc. You haven't told me much at all."

"There is naught to tell. 'Tis only my mother and me. And William is like a brother to me, even though he was only an orphan my mother took in to raise years ago."

"And how about your father?" she asked. "Is he still alive?"

He released his arms from around her and got to his feet, taking a bird into his hands. "You tell me," he said, not even looking at her. "There seems to be secrets in my family that I'm not privy to knowing. Mayhap, you can find out what I cannot."

"I'm sorry," she said, getting to her feet. "I didn't mean to pry." She didn't want to ruin the glorious moods they were both in earlier, so she decided to change the subject. "Please, tell me about your birds."

That seemed to snap him out of his foul mood. A smile crossed his face and he took her hand in his. "Let me show you." He pulled her inside the wooden house that occupied the roof. She was amazed at how much room there was inside.

"There are a lot of birds in here, as well as many outside," she said, looking all around the room.

"Aye," he told her, showing her an enclosed partition that housed about eight birds. "These are my breeders."

"You breed birds?" she asked in surprise.

"I do. They are sitting on eggs now that should hatch in a few days' time." He gently placed his hand on a nesting bird and lifted it slightly so she could see the egg beneath it. "They normally lay two eggs at a time. And the mother and father both take turns sitting on them."

"I like that," she said with a chuckle. "A father who watches after the babies as well."

"The squabs, or chicks, will be ready to be on their own in about thirty days."

"And why are those caged separately?" she asked, pointing to an adjacent room.

"Those are my best flyers," he told her proudly. "They are the ones that belong to the flock back at Brynmawr – my other pen that you've already seen. If I let them out, they will fly straight to their home."

"And they are the ones that carry messages?"

"Aye. I have also raced my flyers in the past to earn coin. The ones that are sitting loose atop the cage have won money for me many times. I would take them to the far edge of town and release them to fly back here. The people of the town have often placed bets for entertainment. The coin earned helps to take care of my family as well as the birds."

"How did you start all this? It seems to me that usually only the nobility have these birds since they are expensive to raise."

He scooped out seed from a barrel to feed the birds, not looking at her when he talked. "I don't think you want to hear it."

"Oh, but I do."

He put the scoop down and looked up. "All right, then," he said and cleared his throat. "You told me about your family. In respect, I will do the same for you. When I was young, I often went to Shrewsbury Castle against my mother's wishes because I was curious."

"Why wouldn't she want you to go? The castle courtyard is open to everyone during the day."

He shook his head and continued caring for the birds. "I don't understand it. But she never wanted me to go near a castle. She and William wouldn't go either. Anyway, when I was about ten we moved here after constantly changing homes at least twice a year. When we came here to . . . trade one day, the master tailor, Dion, took a fancy to my mother."

"Do you mean when you came here to steal?" she asked with a raised brow.

He closed his eyes and released a deep breath. He nodded and then looked right at her. "That was probably why we moved so much through the years," he told her. "But I was young and did whatever my mother needed me to do in order for us to survive. She was a single parent with two young children. You have to realize, if she hadn't taught me to steal, we would all be dead right now."

"I am sorry," she said, still not condoning it, but now understanding him a little more. Her heart went out to him. "Please, continue."

"Dion was a widower with no children of his own," he told her. "So he took us in. He wanted to marry my mother, but she never would for some odd reason. We continued to stay here anyway. I think he was lonely and also always hoped my mother would change her mind and marry him. Dion was well off for a merchant and also a learned man. He had the opportunity to learn to read and write from his own apprenticeship at one time to a tailor who once worked for the nobles. He was kind enough to teach the skills to William and myself, though my mother had no interest in changing."

"Is he the man who lives downstairs?" she asked.

"Aye. He owns the shop."

"I would like to meet him some day," she told him.

Madoc nodded and continued. "William showed interest in Dion's trade and was able to secure an apprenticeship with him. I, on the other hand, learned a little of everything doing odd jobs for the merchants in town, but never mastered anything. You see, we still needed to pay Dion for my brother's apprenticeship. Those are the rules of the guild. My mother took on a job as a weaver for him and, together, we managed to pay what was needed, but 'twas very expensive. Dion let us live here, collecting no rent since my brother was his apprentice. We had to buy our own food, and William had to buy supplies."

"Why wouldn't your mother just marry Dion? Wouldn't that have ended your problems?"

"My mother does things I do not understand, and never will. She is very private and will not disclose things even to her own children," he said with a disgruntled look upon his face. Then, he continued. "After seven years, William became a journeyman and started to receive a small wage. While he wasn't allowed to marry during his apprenticeship, he could have done so while being a journeyman. I think he never did because he felt he had to focus on his craft as well as watch over Mother."

"Is that when you went to work at the castle?"

"Aye. I decided I wanted to be something – someone in life. I wanted to be respected, as was William. I thought by working at the castle, I would accomplish that over time. I loved to watch the lord and his knights and always hoped someday . . . someday that could be me."

"'Tis not all as wonderful as it seems," she pointed out.

"Anything would have been better than what I'd lived through. Or at least I thought it couldn't get any worse at that time."

"So it got worse? What happened?"

"Well, I was able to secure a job helping to tend to the birds in the castle mews. I took a fancy to the pigeons, and they seemed to be drawn to me more than to anyone else. I stayed there for a few years. But one winter food was scarce and they started killing the pigeons for food."

"That is common," explained Abbey. "We eat pigeons at my father's castle quite often." She saw the pained look on his face and knew now she shouldn't have mentioned it. "Did it bother you?" she asked.

"Aye. Very much so. I had considered the birds my own even though they were not. So in order to save their lives, every so often I would leave the castle walls and sneak a bird out of the gates under my cloak.

"I brought them home and built a pen on the roof. Dion liked me, so he looked the other way. I am sure he knew from where they came. I started to breed them and, before long, my numbers multiplied. This went on for some time. But one day, the man I worked with in the mews caught me stealing a bird and turned me in to Lord Shrewsbury."

"And he threw you in the dungeon just like he's done to my brother."

"Aye, he did. And as common treatment of a thief, my hand was dyed red by berries to label me, should I be released. But Lord Shrewsbury was not that kind. And I would have been executed had I not found a way to escape. I had to hide my hand for months in order not to be discovered."

"Did you use a disguise in order to escape the dungeon?"

"Actually, I lured the guard to the door of my cell and without him knowing, I pilfered the keys from his waist. When he fell asleep at his post as he often did, I used the keys to let myself out. I am not proud to say I knocked the man unconscious in order to steal his clothes. But I needed them for the disguise that would allow me to walk out of there without anyone questioning me."

"You are resourceful," she said with a smile and a nod of her head. "Did you kill the guard in the process?"

"Nay. Though my mother trained me to steal, she did not teach me to kill."

A sudden thought went through her head. She'd been so used to seeing all the men at the castle with weapons. Battle and killing was common for them, as well as for her father and brothers. But she just realized she had never seen Madoc hurt or kill anyone. He didn't even carry a weapon with him, except for her dagger that he only used as a tool.

"Madoc," she asked curiously. "Have you ever killed a man?"

He looked over to her and his eyes stared into hers. A sudden sadness lingered in his gaze. He looked to the ground when he answered.

"I may be a thief, but I am not a murderer. And while 'tis common for a titled man or a man-at-arms to carry weapons and to kill, 'tis not for a commoner, like me. I have not killed, my lady, but that does not mean I never will or that I am unable to defend you."

"Of course not." She hadn't meant it in that way and could feel Madoc's insecurities through his words.

"Are you ashamed of me?" he asked. "Ashamed not only that I steal but because I will never be the kind of man you are used to?" He looked at her with eyes that held all the pain of the world within them. She would never tell him she was ashamed of him when he'd already tortured himself with thoughts of his own.

"You did what you had to in order to survive," she said. "And I want you to know that I feel safer with you by my side than with one of my father's guards."

He looked at her and she could tell he was biting the inside of his cheek. Then he turned back to his work as he continued his story.

"Once I escaped from the castle, I was a fugitive. They came looking for me at first, and found my pen of birds. Luckily, Dion was able to convince them that they were his. He was a wealthy merchant and, by law, could own them if he so chose. I do think a few coins exchanged hands, having something to do with their decision to look the other way as well. But that's when I knew I was only endangering my family by staying here. So I decided to leave."

"Is that when you built your hut and other pen in the mountains on the border?"

"Aye. I was on my own and am embarrassed to say that not long ago I ran with a band of marauders. But not anymore. Anyway, I could not stay away from my family forever. So as William became skilled with a needle and thread, he made disguises for me. With these disguises I was able to slip in and out of Shrewsbury without anyone noticing. I couldn't take the chance that one of the townsfolk would turn me in for a reward."

"Oh, so you are a man with a price on your head?"

He didn't answer, making her realize he saw no humor in her words.

"Madoc, I don't want to ever marry Lord Shrewsbury. Mayhap, I will go undiscovered, too, just as you have for all these years."

"Highly unlikely, my lady. While I was only a commoner,

their loss was little. But you are a titled lady and worth more than me. They are looking for you and won't stop until they find you. You are at risk staying here."

"I am also risking the lives of you and your family, aren't I?"

He didn't answer. He just cleaned up and escorted her back out to the roof.

"I would really like to go down to the market," she told him.

He looked at her and shook his head. "Nay, 'tis not a good idea. You might be recognized. I already risked much by letting the guard at the gate see you when we arrived last night. I was hoping he wouldn't see my face in the dark but, unfortunately, he recognized me. I should have taken the time to find a disguise. If I hadn't been in such a hurry to get here before they closed the gates, I would have."

"I will wear my hood over my head," she said. "No one will see my face. Please, I want to experience it."

He helped her down the ladder, his protective arms around her as he descended ahead of her and blocked her body from falling.

"Abbey," he said, tilting her chin up to look into her eyes. "You play with fire. You don't know what you ask."

"But you wear disguises and never get caught," she said.

"That is different. I am a *Lord of Illusion*. A master of what I do."

"I beg you . . . I really want to go."

She could see it in his eyes that he already regretted this, but she knew he would agree to her wishes. With a silent nod of his head, they descended the side stairs and headed down to the street.

CHAPTER 8

*M*adoc walked through the streets of the town with Abbey by his side. She donned the clothes William had made for her, and had the hood up over her head. She smiled more than he'd ever seen her smile before. He knew it was because of the morning they'd spent in bed. Madoc wore a cape with his head covered also, feeling he should have taken the time for some real disguises for both of them. But Abbey was so excited and in such a hurry to see the town, he had let her convince them they would not even be noticed in the crowd.

His scanned the townspeople eyeing her curiously, and gave a smile and small nod in return. Most of the people were the regulars who lived here and he hoped they wouldn't start asking questions. This was too risky being around so many people, but he couldn't deny her when she had actually begged him to bring her here. This meant a lot to her and he didn't want to let her down. Still, he had a feeling in his gut he'd made the wrong decision.

His mother wasn't speaking to him this morning because

he'd made love to the Lady of Blackmore. He didn't regret his action and actually found himself falling hard for Abbey. He would hate to have to send her away, but he couldn't let her stay and endanger his family any longer. He just didn't know how or what he was going to do that wasn't going to break her heart in the process.

"I feel so alive this morning," she told him, walking proudly down the street, holding on to his arm. He felt the same, but didn't admit it. It would only make parting more difficult. "William is a fine tailor. These clothes fit me perfectly."

ABBEY WAS in awe of the busy life of a town. Never before had she experienced anything like this and she took it all in eagerly. 'Twas even more exciting being in the midst of it than it was viewing it from atop the roof.

Each business was marked by a carved wooden sign outside the shop. There was a shoe for the shoemaker, and a knife with a pig above the butcher's door. Over the shop where William worked was a wooden sign with a needle and thread. The town needed the signs with pictures on them since these were commoners that lived here and they could not read or write. The signs served as a guide.

They walked down Butcher's Row and turned the corner to an even narrower street called Fish Street. A wooden fish hung over the door of the shop. A man with blackened teeth ran up to her and stuck a dead fish in her face.

"Fresh fish t'day fer only a penny," he called out.

She jumped back and held her hand over her nose at the

nasty smell. Madoc put his body between them, blocking her from the man.

"Nay," Madoc told him. "And don't be trying to pass off three-day-old fish as fresh, you fishmonger!" He guided Abbey forward.

"Madoc, that was so harsh," she said as they headed away. She kept her head down and looked up at him from under her hood.

"Not everyone in this town is to be trusted," he told her. "That man, I am sure, is trying to make a quick penny on rancid fish that has been discarded."

"Well, mayhap, he is just trying to do what he can in order to survive." Madoc's silence told her he did not take kindly to her comment.

"We're coming to the questionable part of town now. So stay close," he instructed.

A stray, straggly dog ran by, barking at the heels of a boy running quickly with a row of sausages dangling from the package he carried. A huge pig grunted loudly as it made its way toward her, and she froze. Madoc quickly guided her out of its way.

"Fresh pies, buy my fresh fruit pies!" called a woman passing by with the pie raised up to nose level. It smelled delicious and she wondered how it tasted.

"Buy my bread, buy my bread," came another call from a man behind her. The smell of the crusty loaves drifted to her on the breeze.

"Let me make you a pair of shoes," said a man, grabbing at Abbey's cape to lift it up to see her feet.

"Nay!" Madoc commanded, pushing the man away.

So much was happening so fast that Abbey felt lightheaded. Still, she was happy to be walking down the street as a commoner instead of being guarded by her father's men who barely let her step foot off her horse. She was even beginning to get accustomed to the rancid smell of the streets.

She was happy to have Madoc at her side. She understood him more now that he'd told her his story. Her heart opened to him, never having known some of the struggles he'd been through.

Aye, he was a thief, but he only took what he needed to survive. And though the men at the castle thought naught of taking a life, he'd never killed a soul – and even tried to save the lives of pigeons, risking his own life in the process. She had never known anyone like Madoc, and felt a special place for him in her heart. Aye, she knew now that she was falling in love with him.

They strolled past more houses made of wood and some of stone, each having a huge barrel of water out front.

"What are those for?" she asked, pointing to one.

"In case of fire," he explained. "Should fire break out, 'tis the duty of every townsperson to help out. And though the roofs are no longer thatched as they once were, fires still break out often – from carelessness if naught else."

They turned down Tanner Street. As they walked past the tanner's shop, she saw a man giving a haircut out front of a shop next door with scissors on the sign. Foreign merchants set up stalls in the streets and competed for sales from the townsfolk.

"There are so many merchants here already," she said, "I am surprised the foreign merchants are allowed to sell their wares."

"No one is turned away," he explained. "However, the

merchants that are not from this town have to stay outside the gates at the open of the market for two hours to give the locals and guilds a fair chance to sell first."

"Do you think William will be accepted into the guild?" she asked. "The gown he was working on was stitched beautifully."

"He deserves it," agreed Madoc. "He has worked on that gown for months. William is to the point now where he will present his best piece of work to the guild. If his masterpiece is accepted, he will be able to become a master at his craft and even own his own shop. He can then have apprentices working for him, instead."

"That is so exciting. So is his masterpiece the gown I saw on the table last night? Or does he have more like that one? 'Twas so beautiful."

"That is the only one of that quality," he explained. "He saved money for a long time to be able to afford the silk and velvet in that specific color. It means the world to him to succeed, and also to my mother. She is a weaver now, but is getting too old to work. I worry about her. I don't feel she is long for this world. Her body shakes constantly and, lately, she has trouble breathing."

They passed a flower vendor on the street. Abbey didn't see Madoc buy it, but he handed her a flower. The thought crossed her mind that he'd lifted it in secret as they passed the cart. Either way, it was a nice thought on his part and meant the world to her. It was a red tulip, a harbinger to spring. She sniffed it as they walked.

When she started to turn down the next street, Madoc's hand on her shoulder stopped her.

"You don't want to go down Grope Lane," he told her. "That is the alley of ill repute."

She looked down the small, dirty street and saw beggars sitting in the doorways and even a whore standing outside a building with a wine barrel hanging above the door as a sign. She guessed the building to be the local tavern.

"I can guess why it is given that name," she said. By Madoc's laugh, she knew she was correct.

He turned her in the opposite direction down Church Street. A beautiful church with rare, stained glass windows and a tall tower spire with a bell up top, rose up majestically from the end of the street.

"That is St. Alkmund's Church," he told her. "The monks in black robes on the stairs are the Benedictines."

She surveyed the monks in their black robes, hoods raised so you couldn't even see their faces. She thought they reminded her of Madoc the day he'd pretended to be an old man on the road.

People hurried around her, bumping into her in their travels. The streets were crowded and, though she enjoyed it, she wasn't used to being in such close contact. After a while, she felt like everyone walking by either touched her, bumped her, or brushed against her in some way. Anxiety coursed through her.

"Just relax," Madoc told her with a hand on the small of her back. He led her in the direction of the church and out of the midst of the commotion. "I know this is not what you are used to, but it is a common everyday occurrence for people such as me."

Just then, a town crier ran by ringing a hand bell. The young boy cried out the daily news. She wasn't really listening, but stopped dead in her tracks as she heard her name slipping from the boy's lips.

"Lady Abigail from Blackmore's gone missing!" he cried. "Reward, reward! The Lord of Shrewsbury offers three pounds for the return of his betrothed."

"Keep walking," came Madoc's deep voice in her ear. "And keep your head low. We can no longer be out on the street. Now, I am not the only one with a price on my head, am I?"

Abbey knew he hadn't liked her commenting about the price on his head earlier and figured she deserved his remark, though she did not like it.

"'Tis not a price on my head," she retorted. "After all, 'tis not nearly enough considering the size of the dowry I would be bringing to the marriage. And you make it sound as if I'm some sort of criminal."

"Well, what would you call it?" he asked in amusement. "You not only struck a guard and stole his horse, but are a fugitive now that you've joined up with me. You really should choose your acquaintances with more thought behind it."

Abbey looked up and saw Shrewsbury Castle in the distance. She felt a knot forming in her stomach and wanted to go back to a private place and wrap herself in the protection of Madoc's arms.

When Madoc guided her down the street even faster, she realized the castle guards rode through the gates of the town and were talking to the gatekeeper, Barclay. With them, were her two guards from Blackmore. Barclay looked up, scoped the area with a scrutinizing glance, and pointed in their direction.

· · ·

MADOC HURRIED Abbey down the street, knowing now he should have listened to his gut and never brought her out in public. He knew he couldn't trust Barclay. The man eagerly pointed them out from his position atop the watchtower, doing it for the coin the guards offered.

"I see them," called Abbey's guard, Emric, hurrying his horse in their direction. People scattered out of the way, clearing a quick path for the castle's men.

Madoc could see he wasn't going to be able to hide Abbey now. And he'd be hanged for having harbored her. He only hoped they hadn't caused trouble for his mother or William.

"Let's get to the church!" he instructed, grabbing her hand and dragging her along with him. The guards approached just as they reached the steps. He pulled her up behind him, but her skirt got caught around her feet and almost tripped her in the process. The monks scattered out the way, blessing themselves. Then the guards shouted out for them to stop, but Madoc ripped open the door to St. Alkmund's and dragged her inside.

"We are safe in here," he told her.

She looked to him with frightened eyes, struggling to catch her breath. "They won't follow us inside?"

"Nay. We have sanctuary here for forty days. But they will post a lookout to watch for our escape."

He pushed the hood from his head and ran a hand through his hair, pacing back and forth, trying to think. He could see the crowd gathering outside in curiosity. The Shrewsbury Castle guards pranced their horses back and forth, while the guards from Blackmore stood looking up the steps of the church.

"Come out, Lady Abigail," called out the guard named

Desmond. "Come out, or we will be forced to return with news of your escape to your father."

"Hand over the Lady of Blackmore, anon," shouted a Shrewsbury guard.

"What's going to happen?" asked Abbey, trembling. She didn't want to be in this position.

"Oh, naught to worry about," Madoc said sarcastically, still pacing back and forth. "You're just going to marry the ogre and I'll end up in the dungeon for a while before they hang me."

"Nay! They wouldn't do that."

"What did you think would happen when they caught up to us, sweetheart? Did you think they'd throw a celebration and invite us to join them? I have to think of an escape."

"You were right. I never should have come to town today," she said sadly. "I endangered you and your family."

"What would it matter? The gatekeeper saw us come in last night anyway. I'm sure he knows I brought you to my mother's place." He walked away from the door and back into the chapel area, looking for something – anything – that would aid him in their escape. "I have to hurry and warn William and my mother," he called out to her. "If they imprison them too, I'll never forgive myself."

He heard her voice answer from behind him. "I'm so sorry, Madoc. I never meant to put any of you in danger. I'll never forget you. And I truly love you. Goodbye."

Goodbye? She sounded as if she were going somewhere. Then he felt the breeze from the open door and spun on his heel, knowing exactly what she meant.

"Abbey – nay! Come back." 'Twas too late. She'd walked out the door and sealed her fate. No longer would she be protected by sanctuary from the church, nor would he be able to protect her either. He ran to the open door and stopped at the entrance. A guard got off his horse and ran up the stairs to collect Abbey.

He wanted to go after her, but didn't. He wanted to tell her she didn't need to surrender herself to a life of doom and that he would think of a way to protect her and they would escape together. Aye, he wanted to tell her that he . . . loved her?

That thought alone scared him more than all the rest put together. This couldn't be happening. Why was he feeling this way about a lady he could never have? And why had she said she loved him, just to make matters worse? They could never be together and he was only fooling himself if he thought they could. He belonged here, in the smelly streets with the ragpickers and fishmongers. She belonged in a castle with rose water and servants tending to her every wish. Lady Abigail deserved someone better than him. She could never be happy with him, and he needed to let her go.

He stood there in sanctuary, just watching her, but doing naught to help her. The guard put her on the horse and pulled himself up behind her. She looked to Madoc with haunting, sad eyes that burned a hole through him all the way to his very soul. He needed to let her go, he tried to convince himself. Besides, he couldn't go after her now without getting imprisoned. And being in prison was something he never wanted to experience again.

Madoc watched her ride away with the guards, while two guards stayed, anticipating his escape. His heart ached at the choice he had made, but it was over now. There was naught to do but to see to the safety of William and his mother.

He closed the door and went back into the church. The

sun streamed in from the stained glass window, lighting up the crucifix on the wall. It made him feel even worse for the choice he'd made. He thought of Abbey having to marry Lord Shrewsbury and how hard she had tried to escape him. She had seemed so unhappy. A knot formed in his stomach and a cloud fogged over his brain. He no longer knew what was wrong or right. Had he ever known in all his years? Then he spied something else he hadn't noticed before.

He wasn't a praying man by any means, but blessed himself as he walked up to the altar, knowing he was going to hell for certain for what he was about to do.

CHAPTER 9

*A*bbey had gone from being the happiest girl in the world to the saddest in a matter of a day. She rode into the courtyard of Shrewsbury Castle on the guard's horse, feeling like she was going to her death. Her own guards headed back to her father's castle to relay the message that she had been delivered. 'Twould be after the wedding that her brother would be released. The last thing she wanted to do was to surrender, but she had no choice.

'Twas the only thing she could do to give Madoc the time he needed to escape. He was right in saying he would go to the dungeon and be hanged for having harbored her. She also worried for his mother and William. Abbey never meant to endanger anyone when she decided to escape her own fate.

Now, she realized in her selfishness wanting to live a different life, she'd probably ruined others' lives in the process. She was a lady. This was her life, like it or not. Aye, she decided she would go to her death by marrying Lord Shrewsbury if it would save the lives of Madoc and his family.

Abbey would miss Madoc deeply. Her heart already ached for his presence at her side. If only things could be different, she could live the life she wanted with him instead of with the vile Lord Shrewsbury.

"Let me see her!" A low voice split the air. Then, a man she guessed to be the ogre she was to marry, rushed down the steps from the battlements to her side. The guard helped her off the horse. The man from the battlements reached out and touched her face. She cringed under his perusal and closed her eyes.

"Open your eyes and look at me, Wife," shouted the man. Her eyes flew open and she daringly matched his stare.

He was a tall man, mayhap ten years her senior, with dark, curly hair and beady eyes that bore into her with fire. His temples held a hint of gray and his stomach hung out past his belt. He walked with a limp, more or less dragging one of his legs behind him. He might have been a handsome man at one time, but now he was old and broken.

"So, you are the Lady of Blackmore – my bride."

"I am Abigail of Blackmore," she retorted. "But I will never be your bride!"

His hand shot out and slapped her across her face. Her head jerked to the side, but she held her ground. The sting on her cheek bit into her flesh as powerful as the hatred she held for this man.

How could her father have done this to her? Madoc would never think of hurting her, yet not five minutes in this man's presence and he'd already hurt her physically and mentally, too.

"You will be wed to me in less than a sennight," he

growled. "And you will never speak to me in that manner again. Do you understand?"

Abbey toyed with the idea of not answering him or, perhaps, spitting in his face. But the sting on her cheek reminded her that she had naught to gain by those actions and everything to lose.

"Aye, my lord," she answered instead.

"That's better." He reached out and picked up a lock of her hair. "So soft," he said, putting his nose against it to smell it. "And so delicious." Then he reached out and grabbed a hold of her gown at the shoulder. "What are these peasant rags you wear?" He looked over to his guards and shouted. "Get her to her room in the tower and summon her lady-in-waiting. Then call for the tailor and have him make her a proper gown."

"Aye, my lord," answered the guard. "But . . . the tailor died last evening."

"Then go to the town and find another one. And hurry. I don't want her to be seen looking like this. 'Tis an embarrassment to me."

The guard roughly dragged her toward the castle where she spied the stone tower that was to be her chamber and her prison. Why the tower? So high up. She wished more than anything for Madoc to be there to hold her hand and tell her it was going to be all right.

Holding back the tears that threatened to spill forth, she tried not to think of how wonderfully this morning had started and, now, how horribly it would end.

* * *

MADOC SAT in silence during the mass with his head down at the back of the church, trying to hide his face under the hood. He had donned the black robe he'd found hanging on the wall. It was the robe of a Benedictine monk.

Every minute seemed to be an hour. And every second he stayed there was just another chance that his mother and William had already been seized. And he didn't even want to think of what may have happened to Abbey.

Damn it, what in God's name had she been thinking to surrender? He looked up and blessed himself, not sure he wouldn't be struck down dead for thinking blasphemy in church.

Hadn't she heard him tell her to stay in the church and she would have sanctuary? Of course she had. But when had she ever done anything he'd told her to do? He had half a mind to spank her for her silliness if he ever saw her again.

He looked up and blessed himself for that thought, especially since it almost aroused him thinking of putting his hand on her bare behind. At this rate, he'd have to pilfer more coin just to donate it to the church to cleanse him of his sins. However, stealing coins wouldn't help his situation any since he already had no chance in hell of making it to Heaven. Once more, he blessed himself and let out a sigh of relief that mass was finally over. He suddenly remembered why he never came to church in the first place.

Quickly getting to his feet, he silently fell in line with the monks as they exited the church. He kept his hood up and head low, and was glad the monks weren't known for idle chatter. He looked up slightly to see the two guards that stood watch, waiting for him to try to escape. To his relief, they were talking amongst themselves and eating, and only glanced at the monks as they walked by.

Once out of view, he hurried down Grope Lane to take the back way to his abode.

"Oooo, a monk," cooed a whore from the doorway of the tavern. "Come here," she motioned with her finger. A crippled beggar sitting in front of the tavern reached out and grabbed at his cloak. "Alms for the poor?" he asked. Madoc brushed his hand away and continued onward.

He sneaked through the back garden of his home, climbing the stairs quickly. That's when he noticed his birds were still out of the loft. There was no way he could leave them out all night. In one motion he rushed into the loft and opened the top hatch, scattering seed and calling them inside with soft coos from his throat. Luckily, he'd never had trouble getting his birds inside. In a matter of minutes he had them secured and made his way down from the roof and in through the back door.

His mother sat at the table, her face more ashen than yesterday. William was finishing up the gown of silk and velvet. He cut the thread and let out a sigh.

"All finished." He held it up for his mother to see just as Madoc made his entrance.

His mother glared at him as he walked in to join them. "What have you done?"

William looked over and smiled and nodded. "Good disguise, Brother. When I heard you and Lady Abigail were in the church, I knew you'd have a plan of escape."

Madoc put a hand on his mother's shoulder. "I'm sorry to have endangered you two by bringing her here," he said. "But Abbey has surrendered and they've taken her to the castle."

"What do you plan on doing?" asked William, admiring the gown he had made that was fit for a lady. The color of the cloth was expensive and he handled it carefully so as not to soil it.

"I am going after her," he said without thinking about it.

"Nay," answered his mother. "You stay away from the castle. Just let her be."

Madoc removed his borrowed robe, satisfied that his family was safe. If the guards hadn't sought them out by now, they probably wouldn't come after them. Or at least not until they discovered his escape.

He sat down next to his mother and took her hands in his. "Mother. You mean the world to me and always will. I could never defy the woman who bore me, and I thank you for all you have sacrificed for me over the years. But while at mass, I thought about this a lot. I know I should just let her go, but I can't. I have to go after her. Don't you understand?"

"You attended mass?" William asked with a chuckle to his voice. "You really have changed since you've met her."

Madoc ignored him, concentrating instead on his mother and the way his words seemed to make her tense up in his arms. She had been acting very odd ever since he'd brought Abbey home.

"I don't want to lose you," she told him. He could see the sorrow in her eyes as well as fear.

"But I've been in many dangerous situations in my life and have always come back to you, Mother. I've always returned home."

Once again, she tensed and pulled her hand away from his.

"Then do what you will, Madoc. We all make mistakes we

have to live with. Just remember whatever you choose will haunt you for the rest of your life."

She wasn't making any sense. He glanced over to William, but his brother looked the other way. Madoc didn't know what was going on, but he'd had enough of this.

"Mother, is there a secret you've been keeping from me my entire life?"

Her eyes sprang open wide and she glared at William. William gave a small shake of his head and walked away to clean up his sewing.

"Is my father truly dead?" he asked. "Or are you lying?"

Her face remained stone-like. "I can honestly say that your father is dead," she replied.

"And what did he do for a living and how did he die? And why won't you ever tell me anything about him?"

He heard William clear his throat and noticed that his mother could not look him in the eye.

"I feel weak and need to go to my room," she said. It was her way of avoiding his question once again. It angered him but, at the same time, he didn't have the time to pursue it. He had to spend the night devising a way to get inside the castle since he planned on being there to save Abbey first thing in the morning.

His mother went to her room as Madoc paced the floor. He ran a weary hand through his hair, having no idea what he was going to do. William continued to admire his finished gown.

"I was going to present this to the guild tomorrow," William told Madoc. "But then a messenger from the castle came to our door."

"A messenger?" Madoc stopped pacing and his head jerked

up. "What did he want? Did they say you and Mother were to be punished?"

"On the contrary," answered William, running his hand over the gown. "He said Lord Shrewsbury requires a tailor to come to the castle first thing in the morning. It seems they need someone to sew a gown for Lady Abigail."

"Really?" Madoc cradled his chin in thought, his other hand under his elbow. "So . . . is Dion going then?" He referred to his mother's boyfriend. "After all, he is the master of the craft."

"Nay. Dion left for the coast this morning to meet a ship with fine silks coming in to trade. He won't be back until late on the morrow." William placed the gown on the table, flicking off invisible specks of lint. He was so proud of it, and should be. The gown was his best piece of work yet.

"Are you going to the castle then?" asked Madoc.

"Aye, 'tis my duty." William nodded his head. "I told the messenger to tell Lord Shrewsbury I'd be there at dawn tomorrow."

"Nay, you won't," said Madoc, having a sudden idea. This could be his answer. "I will go in your place."

William looked up, very confused. "But you cannot sew, Madoc. Even if it gets you in the castle gates, if you can't produce a gown for the lady, you will be thrown into the dungeon. You cannot risk it."

Madoc's eyes fastened on the gown William was holding up in front of himself in admiration.

"But I will be able to produce a gown," he told him.

"How?" William's eyes followed Madoc's gaze and a look of horror washed over his face. "Nay, you cannot take my gown." He held it to his chest protectively. "I have worked on this for months. 'Tis my ticket to a better life and a shop of my own."

Madoc smiled. "I hope you don't plan on sleeping tonight," he told William. "Because I am going to need a cape and head-dress to go along with it."

CHAPTER 10

*M*adoc walked up to the castle with a bag of thread, needles, and scissors under his arm. He had another bag with the gown, cape, and headdress clutched in his hand. He'd felt bad about taking William's masterpiece. But once he had explained to his brother that he loved Abbey and needed to do everything in his power to save her, William had reluctantly surrendered his best work into Madoc's eagerly awaiting hands.

It only made his mother more upset than she'd been the day before, but Madoc hadn't the time to discover the seed of her anger. He had no trouble getting out of town and past the soldiers who still sat guarding the church – the fools. Dressed in William's attire, the gatekeeper had been tricked by his appearance as well.

He stood now at the castle gate as they were just raising the portcullis for the day. The villeins stood in line with baskets, waiting to use the castle's kitchen to bake their bread. The gate lifted, and the castle's steward was there to greet them.

"Is the tailor from town amongst you?" he asked.

"Aye," said Madoc, pushing to the front of the crowd. The steward had a piece of parchment in his hand.

"William ap Powell?" he read off. "Journeyman to the master tailor, Dion of Shrewsbury?"

"Aye," he answered again, keeping his head low.

"Follow me," said the man. The steward led him to the great hall where they were joined by a large man with angry eyes. "Lord Shrewsbury," the man said with a slight bow. "The town's tailor is here at your request."

Madoc had vaguely known Lionel in the short time he'd worked at the castle, and only hoped the man did not remember him. Still, he kept his face turned down in precaution.

"Tailor," boomed the lord's loud voice. "Ap Powell . . . do I know that name from somewhere?"

"Wasn't that the name of the boy from the village years ago who worked in the mews?" The steward supplied the information. Madoc could have hit him.

"Aye, I do believe you are correct," said the lord cocking his head to look at Madoc.

"'Twas my brother," mumbled Madoc, hoping they would believe him. "He died in a dungeon in Scotland last year."

"Dungeon?" asked the lord. Madoc cursed himself for saying that, as it probably only reminded the man of where he'd ended up while there. "What was he imprisoned for?"

"I . . . I'm not sure," he replied. "But I'm sure it was just a misunderstanding."

"Lord Shrewsbury?" came a woman's voice and Madoc was glad for the interruption. "Shall I take the tailor to measure my lady for her gown?" A petite woman with auburn hair piled atop her head stood waiting for the lord's approval.

"Aye," he said, his attention taken from Madoc. "I want my betrothed to have the best gown ever for our wedding."

"Wedding gown?" Madoc had not known this was to be a wedding gown. The gown in his bag was bright reddish-orange, not the color expected for a ceremony. "I thought I was to make clothes for her to wear around the castle."

"You'll do that, too," he said. "And I'll expect you to stay until the task is completed."

"Of course, my lord." He bowed and followed the lady-in-waiting up the tower stairs.

"Is this where they're keeping her? Way up here?" he asked the woman, climbing higher and higher.

"'Tis where Lord Shrewsbury wants her. I do believe he's afraid she will escape, so he wants her high in the tower."

"Escape? I thought they were to be married."

"Aye," she answered. "But my lady wants naught to do with my lord, and has made it quite clear."

Madoc smiled at that, thinking how no one could make Abbey do anything she didn't want to do.

"Here we are," she said, using her key to unlock the door.

It angered him to see that Abbey was a prisoner. She didn't deserve this, and he would help her escape just as soon as he could.

The woman walked into the room and Madoc followed. Abbey was lying on the bed and jumped up when they entered. A smile crossed her face when she saw him. He was sure she was going to shout out his name.

"I am William," he told her, his eyes darting back to the

maid. "I am the tailor from town and here to measure you for your wedding gown."

A frown crossed her face when she'd heard the word wedding. "You may leave now," Abbey said to the maid, but the woman shook her head.

"I cannot leave a man alone with you in your chamber. 'Tis not customary, and the lord would not like it."

Madoc was becoming impatient. He wanted to be alone to talk to Abbey and needed to get rid of the woman quickly.

"Oh, I forgot my sewing bag down in the great hall," he said, hiding the bag behind his back. "Will you get it for me, please?" he asked her with a smile.

"I am Lady Abigail's lady-in-waiting. I cannot leave her alone with you."

"'Tis fine," Abbey reassured her. Then she held out an empty flagon. "And would you please stop by the buttery and see that this is refilled with wine?"

"I can call a page for that, my lady. I am here to see to your other needs."

Madoc decided to take this into his own hands. He pushed back his hood and gave her his best smile. He'd never had trouble getting any woman to do what he wanted once he turned on the charm. He let his eyes scan down her body. "You do look comely today. What is your name?"

"I am Lady Bernadette," she said, her face reddening.

"I truly appreciate your help and will be looking forward to seeing you more throughout my stay. Are you perhaps married?"

She looked at him and then back to Abbey, shifting from foot to foot uncomfortably. Then she snatched the flagon away from Abbey, curtseyed quickly and rushed out the door.

Abbey laughed, but Madoc held a finger to his lips to silence her. After checking outside the door that the girl had gone, he came back to Abbey. He tossed the bags on the bed, pulled her into his arms and pressed his lips to hers in a passionate kiss. When the kiss lingered, she motioned to him that she needed to breathe and he let her out of his embrace.

"Madoc, I am so happy to see you!" she exclaimed.

"Why the hell did you leave the church when I told you to stay?"

"I had to. If I didn't, they would have come for you and, mayhap, your family."

"Well, they're still waiting for me outside the church," Madoc told her. "But as soon as they realize their mistake, they'll be after me again."

"How did you manage to escape?"

"It doesn't matter." He went to the tower window and looked out. They were at the highest point in the castle. What bad luck. There weren't even any vines to climb down the walls with and the only thing below them was the moat.

"'Tis going to be hard to scale this wall, but with some ropes . . ."

"I am not going out the window," she told him, cutting him off from saying more. "'Tis too high."

"Oh, that's right. You are afraid of heights." He rolled his eyes and shook his head. Looking out the adjoining window, he realized there was a battlement not far down. "Mayhap if we –"

"Nay," she snapped, cutting off his words again. "We'll just have to think of something else."

"We haven't much time," he explained. "Your lady-in-waiting will be back soon."

He pulled her into his arms again, and she cried softly as she laid her head against his chest.

"Oh, Madoc, I am so sorry this had to happen. And now I am to be married in a few days to a man I do not love." She turned her head and, when she did, he noticed the red welt across her cheek. Anger boiled within him that anyone would touch her in such a way.

"Did that bastard hit you?" he growled in a low voice. "I will kill him for hurting you, I swear I will."

"Nay." She grabbed his arm tightly. "You must not bring any attention to yourself. You told me that you once worked here and stole from his father. If they recognize you, then . . ."

"They won't," he said. "I assure you of that. I will be staying right under their noses, yet they won't know 'tis me."

"For your sake, I hope you are right," she said.

"Aye," he mumbled, trying to come up with a plan. "And so do I."

CHAPTER 11

"You want me to do what?" asked William with a bewildered look upon his face.

"Make me a wedding gown," said Madoc.

Madoc had snuck back into town after spending a sleepless night at the castle. Lord Shrewsbury had given him his own chamber only because he wanted the gown completed quickly, and also a quiet place for his tailor to work undisturbed. For this, he was thankful. However, the man hadn't been happy when Madoc didn't join him for dinner. Madoc had faked his own illness in order not to have to go down to dine with the man at his request. He would have liked to have spent the night in Abbey's room, but the guards at her door put an end to that idea quickly.

"I have no supplies to use to make a lady's wedding gown," explained William. "'Twould take me time to come up with the fabric alone."

"That's fine," said Madoc sitting at the table and helping himself to bread and fruit that were spread out to break the fast. He tore off a chunk of dark, coarse bread and chewed as he talked. "Take your time. I don't need it for another few days."

"What!" William paced the room in their home, much the same way Madoc usually did. "It took me months to make the dress you already stole from me. Not to mention, a year to save money enough to buy the fabric."

"I did not steal it," Madoc replied, pouring himself a cup of ale. "You gave it to me."

"Against my will."

"If it'll make you feel better, it fits Abbey perfectly and she loves it."

William's eyes opened wide. "You already gave it to her? Please tell me that isn't so. And do not tell me that Lord Shrewsbury thinks you can make a gown of that quality in naught but a day."

"She really needed something to wear," he told him. "I didn't see the harm in it."

"Nay. I can't do it," protested William crossing his arms over his chest. "I have no material suitable for the wedding of the Lady of Shrewsbury."

Madoc eyed him, then pushed some crumbs around the table with his fingers. He knew his brother would not like his next suggestion. "You said yourself that Dion would be returning with some fine silks later today."

"Nay," said William shaking his head furiously. "You cannot expect me to steal Dion's wares."

"You won't be stealing. Just tell him it is needed for the Lady of Blackmore's wedding gown. It won't be a lie. I am sure Lord Shrewsbury will pay well . . . eventually." Naught had been said about wages but, then again, Madoc wasn't used to paying and was not even thinking about it.

"Dion will be back later today," said William. "But I will not ask him. He will know something is amiss when I am constructing the gown here instead of at the castle."

Madoc picked up a pear and took a bite. If William hated his last idea, he really wasn't going to like the next one at all.

"You are so right. And I was thinking. That is . . . I think you should be the one to go to the castle to sew. After all, I really am worthless when it comes to the craft."

"You try my patience, Madoc! First you tell me you will go in my place and now you want me to go? 'Tis too late. They have already seen you and we will not be able to deceive them."

"Actually, I made certain they did not get a good look at me. I kept my hood up and didn't go to the great hall for dinner. I can sneak you in and no one will be the wiser."

"He is not going!" Their mother stood in the doorway of her room, her arms crossed over her chest. "Madoc, your silly games are going to get us all killed."

"Mother." Madoc rushed over to her and helped her to the table. She looked worse today and it was obvious her health was dwindling quickly. "I am only trying to help Abbey."

"That girl is nothing to us, so leave her be."

"Nay, you are wrong, Mother. I feel something for her that I have felt for no other woman. And I have decided that if I can save her from Lord Shrewsbury, I am going to ask her to marry me."

"Marry you?" both William and his mother said together.

"Aye. I love her."

His mother shook her head and squeezed her eyes closed. "You are only a commoner, Madoc. You have no right to think you can marry nobility."

"Mother, mayhap we should –" William started but was cut off by his mother's hand in the air.

"William, you will not help Madoc with his deceitful actions. Do you hear me?"

The room was quiet and no one spoke. Then William, for the first time that Madoc could ever remember, challenged his mother.

"Nay, Mother. You are wrong, and I *will* help him. You are the one I will no longer help with your lies. I can do it no more."

Madoc didn't understand what was happening. All he knew was that his mother was hiding something from him, and William was going to help him save Abbey.

The church bell rang loudly from outside their window. They could hear the noise of the street below. People were shouting and something wasn't right. Madoc ran to the front window to see Barclay bolting out of the church, the louse. He could hear him telling the castle guards about the escape.

"Let's go," Madoc told William. "I need to get you into the castle before they find me."

William hurried around the room, collecting up his things. Then he pulled on a cloak and lifted the hood up over his head.

"Mother," said Madoc. "Can we count on you to tell Dion of William's whereabouts when he returns?"

She didn't answer and neither did she look at Madoc. It hurt him that she would reject him this way. He had always done whatever he could for her, but she had never liked the fact that he wouldn't always listen to her wishes. But he couldn't. He was a free spirit who had to live by his own decisions. And whatever the secret was that she'd been keeping from him his entire life, he could see it was finally coming between them.

"Let's go then," Madoc said to William, placing a kiss on his mother's cheek. He could see the tears she held back and didn't want to leave her this way. But he had no choice. He had to go. He had to save Abbey.

They were to the door and about to step out when he heard his mother's voice from behind him.

"Please be careful," she told them. "I will talk to Dion when he returns. And I will get the chandler's young son to watch after your birds."

"Thank you, Mother," said Madoc, feeing a sense of relief.

"Promise me that you will return."

"I promise," he said, and turned and left the room.

*　*　*

ABBEY RAN TO THE WINDOW, hearing the warning bell of St. Alkmund's Church ringing frantically. Something was wrong. The town was in the distance but she could feel it in her heart that Madoc was in trouble.

When he'd brought the dress to her this morning, he'd told her he was going to sneak back home. She loved the fact he was trying to help her, but it made her worried for him. So worried that she hadn't even been able to sleep.

The key turned in the lock and her lady-in-waiting, Bernadette, walked in.

"Oh, I was coming to assist you in dressing, but I see you've already donned your new gown," said Bernadette. "My, that tailor is fast. And he does wonderful work. The gown in beautiful!"

"Aye, isn't it the finest work you've ever seen?" Abbey couldn't stop admiring the bright, reddish-orange, velvet bodice with small pearls used as buttons trailing down the back. The long sleeves felt so soft and gave way to veils, or tippets, fluttering down from her wrists. The skirt was made of silk, and flowed when she walked across the floor. And small, embroidered flowers scaled the collar line, coming to a deep "v" between her breasts. She had a headpiece of white and orange ribbon interwoven with her hair. The cape that matched lay thrown over the bed.

"I cannot wait until he finishes the wedding gown. You are going to look so beautiful." Bernadette's eyes lit up as she perused the gown.

The wedding was something Abbey didn't want to think about. She could only hope Madoc would come back soon since she didn't want to be anywhere near here come the wedding day.

"The lord calls for you to join him in the great hall for the meal," the woman informed her.

"I really do not want to go," she told Bernadette. "Last night was horrible and I couldn't wait to leave his side."

"You will come to like him in time," she said, walking over to the dressing table. She picked up a brush and ran it through the ends of Abbey's hair. "That is, unless you fancy someone else."

"I know not of what you speak," said Abbey.

"I noticed the way you looked at that handsome, young tailor. I rather fancy him myself."

Abbey didn't know what to say. The woman had seen right through their charade. If she had, so would others. Abbey didn't want her asking more questions so she decided to go down to the great hall, after all. The last thing she wanted to do was to anger Lord Shrewsbury again and end up with another welt across her face.

"Let's go to the great hall," she told her lady-in-waiting. "And please do not say I fancy anyone again – especially not in front of Lord Shrewsbury."

"Aye, my lady. I understand."

Abbey took her place at the dais, standing to the right of her husband-to-be. How she longed to be back home at her own castle instead of here. Mayhap then she'd be able to talk to her father and convince him not to make her marry this awful man.

"My, you look ravishing in that new gown." Lord Shrewsbury held out his arm and she reluctantly took it. He faced her toward the rest of the castle's occupants who were eagerly awaiting his word to start the meal.

"My new bride-to-be," he told them, putting her on display. The people all cheered before he motioned for everyone to sit.

How many times was he going to do this? Last night was enough with the toasts to her beauty after every course. She never thought she'd welcome the rude manners of Madoc, but now she longed for them instead of this. Finally, they were seated and the ewerer came by with water and a basin that they would all use to wash their hands. Then the cupbearer filled each of their cups to the brim with a dark, dry wine.

"Are you enjoying your meal, my darling?" he asked.

She smiled and nodded, not wanting to answer the man.

"Your tailor has done a wonderful job on your gown. I would like to thank him personally but I do not see him here anywhere." He raised his hand in the air and called for a page.

When the boy ran over, he leaned over the table to talk to him. "Please, go at once to the tailor's chamber and tell him I request his presence at my table. And make certain he knows I will not excuse another absence as I did last night."

"Aye, milord." The page ran off while Abbey's heart picked up a beat.

"I thought the tailor was feeling ill, my lord. Perhaps 'twould be better if he joined us at a later time," she said, trying to cover for Madoc.

"I will not hear of it. I have been wanting to speak with him." Lord Shrewsbury lifted his goblet and chugged down some wine.

The page was gone long. Abbey picked at her food and waited anxiously, wondering what Madoc was going to do. She wasn't even sure he was back from town yet or, for that matter, if he'd been captured since she had heard the warning bells earlier.

"Ah, 'tis about time the tailor arrived." Lord Shrewsbury looked over to the entrance of the great hall. Then he stood, waiting for Madoc to join them. Abbey could not even look, not wanting to give away Madoc's identity.

"Come. Sit next to Lady Abigail," said Shrewsbury, motioning with his hand for Brother Andrew to give up his seat. The monk blessed himself and hurried away from the table. Abbey still didn't look up, nor did Madoc say a word. When he seated himself next to her, she finally looked over and almost choked on her food. Instead of Madoc, there sat William, with a scared look upon his face.

While the lord busied himself ordering the kitchen maid to bring more food, Abbey whispered behind her hand.

"William, what are you doing here?"

123

"He is here because I requested his presence," said Shrewsbury, having overheard her. He sat back down at her left side. Abbey was thankful she hadn't mentioned Madoc's name. They might have managed to fool Shrewsbury, but his hearing was excellent.

"The gown you made for my wife is brilliant," he told William.

The look on William's face changed from insecure to proud when he heard that.

"Aye? Do you really think so?" he asked. The kitchen maid put more food down on the table in front of him.

"I do. You are a true master of your trade," Shrewsbury praised him.

William smiled from ear to ear. Confidently, he grabbed a leg of mutton and three carrots and placed them on his trencher.

"Why, thank you kindly." William proceeded to place a rosemary sprig atop his food, and held out the empty cup in front of him, motioning for the cupbearer to fill it. He brought the cup to his mouth but stopped abruptly when he heard the man's next words.

"And so fast! You are faster than any tailor I've ever known."

"I . . . I . . ." he looked to Abbey for help. Abbey shrugged her shoulders slightly, not knowing what to tell him.

"That is good," Shrewsbury continued. "I will be expecting the same quality – nay, better – in the wedding dress you will deliver in three days' time."

William put down the cup and pushed the trencher away from him. He looked as if he were going to be sick. Abbey felt sorry for the man since she knew how long he'd worked on this gown and how impossible it was to complete a gown of this quality in such a short time. This was all Madoc's fault.

"And," continued the lord, holding a finger in the air. "My tailor died and, to my knowledge, had no suitable cloth in his possession. But, I would expect you have your own coffers full by the looks of the gown Lady Abigail is wearing. Therefore, make certain you have all your supplies sent to the castle first thing on the morrow."

"Well, I . . . what I mean is . . ." William's face turned pale.

Abbey could not stand to see William fidget anymore so she broke into the conversation. "Shall we dance, my lord?" she asked, already feeling the knot in her stomach for suggesting this. "I do hear the musicians in the gallery testing their drums and tuning their lutes preparing for the first dance."

"Aye." Shrewsbury seemed pleased by her suggestion. "My leg is twisted from battle, but I can still partake in the dance for a short while. Besides, I would not ignore the musicians after they have been practicing so fervently for the Easter celebrations which will be here soon."

Abbey took his hand as he led her to the floor. When she glanced back over her shoulder, she saw the look of relief on William's face. He gave a small nod of appreciation.

The music started up, drums leading the rhythm, and bells adding an ethereal quality to the song. When the knights noticed their lord had already made his way to the floor to dance before dinner was even over, they instructed everyone to get up and move the trestle tables to make room for them. Grumbles went up from the occupants of the hall, but they did as told. In a matter of minutes, there was a wide, open space in the center of the room and a hundred eager eyes watching them. In her eagerness to help William, she'd only put herself in a horrible position.

Shrewsbury took her hand in his as the music started up and they began their dance.

"Easter," she said aloud, having forgotten all about it since she'd been so preoccupied with Madoc. "Forgive me, my lord, but what day is this? I seem lightheaded from the wine and cannot remember."

"'Tis Saturday," he said. "I expect you to accompany me to mass on the morrow. I am only glad the tailor was able to make you a gown in time."

She was on the lord's right, as was proper for the lady. They started with a Basse dance that was popular with the court. With her left hand held high in his right, they moved forward slowly in a form of a walk as they made their way across the hall. He limped slightly.

"So then," she said nonchalantly. "Four days from now will be Ash Wednesday."

"Aye," he answered. "And on Shrove Tuesday we will be married."

Now she knew why he wanted to rush the marriage. The law stated that during the forty days of Lent, no marriages are to be allowed. So he was hurrying to accomplish the nasty deed before the church made him wait until after Easter.

The music changed, picking up in speed. Other couples joined them in dance on the floor. Shrewsbury moved with small, jerking actions, but still feasible for having an injury. The partners bowed toward each other, then turned toward the person next to them to do the same. As she curtseyed slightly to her neighbor, the man spoke to her quietly.

"You look like you're enjoying yourself too much for a girl who says she doesn't want to get married."

She looked up in surprise to see Madoc standing in front of her. He was dressed like a noble in fine clothes. He had his long hair tied back in a queue and he was wearing a fake mustache. His hair was much lighter than usual. She was sure he had used some sort of powder to make it look that way. But his clear, green eyes let her know 'twas really him.

Abbey almost cried out when she saw him, but bit her tongue. She had to turn back to Lord Shrewsbury before she could answer. But after a spin, she again faced him and they doubled forward, meeting their left shoulders. Doubling back, they repeated the same on the right side.

"I abhor him," she told Madoc softly. "I only suggested the dance to help take the attention away from William."

"Well, I do not like the attention being shared between you and Shrewsbury."

She left him once more and turned back to her lord.

"What is it you are speaking about with that man?" Shrewsbury asked, peering in Madoc's direction.

"'Tis naught, my lord," she told him quickly. "He just . . . gave his congratulations on our betrothal."

Once again, her footing brought her back to Madoc.

"What were you just speaking of with Shrewsbury?" Madoc asked, glaring over at the man.

"If I may say, you do sound as if you are jealous." Abbey arched her eyebrows and smiled slightly. "And where, pray tell, did you get those clothes?"

Madoc's attire looked so unnatural and uncomfortable on him that she almost laughed aloud. Abbey wasn't used to seeing him looking like a noble, dressed in parti-colored hose and pointed shoes. Abbey and Madoc clasped each other's left arms at the elbows and turned in a circle. "And where did you learn to dance?" she asked.

"Never mind that," he said. "Make an excuse to go to your chamber."

They repeated the same step on the right side now.

"I cannot," she told him. "I am in the middle of a dance!"

She turned back and took Lord Shrewsbury's hand, noticing the frown on the man's face. He looked over her shoulder at Madoc and she could see that he, too, was jealous. How did she get into the middle of this?

"I do not recall seeing that man in the castle before. Who is he?"

"I know not, my lord," she said as they bowed toward each other again. "I am merely dancing but I will ask him if 'tis to your liking."

"Please do."

She turned back toward Madoc again, and he was no longer smiling either.

"My lord requests your name," she told him.

"*Your* lord?" Madoc looked over her head. "The lucky sot," he mumbled under his breath. Then he spoke so she could hear him. "It sounds as if you are claiming him. The man is so far into his cups that he can barely stand."

"He is wounded, not drunk," she explained. "Now, stop this nonsense and start concentrating. If we can stall the wedding by just a day, by law we will have to wait for forty days until the end of Lent before we're wed."

Once again, she turned and was back in Lord Shrewsbury's grasp.

"I do not like the way that man stares at me," he said. "I think I shall have him removed from my hall anon."

Before he could carry out his action, Abbey bent down, pretending to twist her ankle. Lord Shrewsbury reached out to help her.

"Please, my lord, if you could just take me back to the table." She glanced over at Madoc who seemed concerned at first that she might have really hurt herself. Then when she motioned with her eyes for him to leave, he understood. He started to walk away until he heard the lord's next words.

"Nonsense," Shrewsbury bellowed. "If you are hurt, I will take you right to your chamber."

There was fire burning in Madoc's eyes now. He looked like he wanted to start a fight. What was the matter with him?

"Nay. Please just call for my lady-in-waiting," Abbey told her betrothed. "The tower stairs are high and I know your leg must be tired from dancing."

That seemed to get his mind off of Madoc. When he agreed, she breathed a sigh of relief. And when she next looked over to where Madoc stood – he was heading through the crowd.

With just a nod of Shrewsbury's head, Abbey's lady-in-waiting came forward to join them. Then the man decided to focus his attention on William who was just finishing up his meal at the dais table.

"Ap Powell," he called out across the hall. "I would have a word with you."

Abbey looked up to see Madoc leaving the room. When Shrewsbury called out, he stopped and slowly turned around at hearing his name. She caught his attention and shook her head, motioning over toward William. Thankfully, Lord Shrewsbury did not notice.

A very nervous William looked up, cup in his hand as he was just starting to drink. His eyes met Lord Shrewsbury's, and then darted over to Abbey in a desperate act of silent pleading for help.

"If I may, my lord," Abbey interrupted. "I was hoping the tailor could help my lady-in-waiting in giving me a hand upstairs. I do not want to put much weight on my hurt foot, and a man's strong arms would be appreciated."

"Nonsense," he said with a shake of his head. "I will summon a page to assist you or, perhaps, one of my men."

He raised a hand and looked around the room. "Page," he called to a young boy.

William's eyes grew frantic. Abbey was not certain he wouldn't swoon like a girl from all the anxiety coursing through him. He most certainly was not fearless to be able to look danger in the eye the way his brother did.

"As you wish, my lord," she said. "However, I was hoping to discuss with the tailor my ideas for the wedding gown. But I suppose it would do no harm in waiting until the morrow."

"What?" That got his attention. "Nay, 'twould not suffice to wait. I want to see the progress on the gown by the end of the day come the morrow." He dismissed the page and, instead, called for William. "Tailor, you will see to my wife's needs. Help her above stairs and listen to her commands in constructing the wedding gown."

"Aye," William squeaked out, jumping to his feet. He got up from the table so quickly that his chair knocked into the cupbearer bringing him more wine. The boy stumbled backwards into a serving wench, falling atop her as he knocked her to the ground. "I . . . I apologize," William stuttered, meaning to help them to their feet.

"Ap Powell," barked Shrewsbury. "They are servants, now leave them be and assist my wife, anon!"

Abbey hated when he called her his wife. She wanted to correct him, but thought better of it. After all, it would only mean trouble for her and, right now, she needed to rescue William. William rushed to her side just as her lady-in-waiting, Bernadette, looked up. Lord Shrewsbury directed his comment to her.

"The tailor will help you take my wife to her chamber now."

Bernadette looked at William with a puzzled look upon her face. "Another tailor? What, my lord, happened to the one I showed to her room yesterday?"

Abbey's heart raced. Bernadette was about to ruin everything. She couldn't let that happen. William looked at the lady-in-waiting and his face turned white.

"Lady Bernadette," Abbey said, placing her hand on the woman's arm. "This is the same man you met yesterday."

"Nay," she said, shaking her head. "I would have remembered that handsome face."

"What is the meaning of this?" ground out Lord Shrewsbury, taking a closer look at William. "Are you the same tailor or not?"

Abbey realized that he really didn't know. Madoc had been careful to keep his hood covering his face, yet careless around Bernadette.

"He is," interrupted Abbey. "He is the man who made the beautiful gown I am wearing."

"I am," William said with a nod of his head.

Then Abbey turned to her lady-in-waiting. "I am sure you are confused, Bernadette. After all, the tailor's face was in shadow under his hood yesterday. Perhaps, you made a mistake." She looked to Bernadette with pleading in her eyes, hoping the woman would understand.

Bernadette looked at her and then over at William. Slowly, she nodded and answered. "Aye, that is correct, my lady. He is the same man as yesterday, I just . . . made a mistake, that's all."

Lord Shrewsbury seemed to accept her answer for now. When he became distracted by a noble trying to gain his favors by praising him in public, Abbey used the opportunity to slip away.

With William on one side and Bernadette on the other, they helped her up the stairs whether she needed it or not. Once they got to the door and Bernadette turned the handle to open it, Abbey walked in first followed by the other two.

Madoc stood at the window and turned around as they entered.

"Oh!" Abbey cried out in surprise. Then she hurried over to him, happy to see him.

"My lady, your foot seems to have healed quickly." Bernadette eyed up Madoc. "You are the tailor I met yesterday," she said suspiciously.

"William, close the door," Abbey instructed. Then she pulled the woman closer to her. "Lady Bernadette, you have to promise you won't mention a word of this to Lord Shrewsbury. If he knew, he would beat me. We would all be in great danger."

"I don't know what is going on," said Bernadette. "I don't like it."

"Please," said William, going to her side. "Allow me to

introduce myself. I am William ap Powell, and also the tailor who made Lady Abigail's gown." He lowered the hood from his head.

Bernadette looked at him curiously and then back to Madoc. "And what about you?" she said. "Why did you pretend to be someone you are not?"

Madoc pulled off his mustache and threw it out the window. He then proceeded to brush the power from his hair. "I am sorry for the deception," he told her sincerely. "But I am trying to save Lady Abigail from marrying a man she loathes."

Abbey cringed when he said the words, not knowing how Bernadette would react. But the secret was out now and they couldn't take it back. They would know in a minute if it would play out or not.

"I see." Bernadette's eyes flashed back to Abbey. "You two are in love and would do anything you can to be together." A small smile turned up the sides of her mouth.

Abbey's heart beat wildly, and she bit her lip. Would Madoc say he loved her in front of the woman?

"Can I count on you to keep our secret?" Madoc asked, not giving an answer one way or the other. Bernadette didn't look like she was going to agree, but then William stepped in to help.

"My Lady Bernadette," he said with a slight bow. "If I may so boldly ask, are you perhaps the wife of one of the castle's knights?"

"Why, no," she answered, seeming flustered. Her hands went to her chest. "I am a maid of honor – unmarried."

"Then allow me to say, you have the most beautiful eyes. I would love to construct a gown to suit you someday, even though it could never surpass your beauty." He picked up her hand and kissed it, causing her face to flush.

"You are even more gallant than your imposter," Bernadette said, talking about Madoc. "And though 'tis against my better judgment, I will keep your secret for now. I will do it because I like the three of you. But if trouble occurs, I cannot keep my promise."

"My gratitude could never be enough," said William, his eyes fastened to her.

"I will leave now," she said, heading toward the door. Then stopping to look over her shoulder, she spoke once more to William. "If I might ask, are you married, William?"

"Nay," he answered. "I am not."

She smiled and opened the door. "Perhaps, I will accept that offer of a gown after all." With that, she silently slipped out of the room, closing the door behind her.

Abbey breathed a sigh of relief. "That could have gone very wrong."

"Aye," answered Madoc, pacing the floor. "'Twas my own carelessness that almost got us discovered. I never should have let her see my face."

"William," said Abbey. "I do believe you have a way with the Lady Bernadette."

"Do you think so?" he asked with a smile. "I rather fancy the woman."

"He learned everything from me," grumbled Madoc. "Now, dear brother, I thank you for the help in our situation, but you need to concentrate on making Abbey's wedding gown."

"Aye." William's eyes were once again filled with fear. "Lord Shrewsbury has ordered me to bring in my own cloth for the gown. Madoc, I need you to go home and convince Mother to get the materials from Dion. 'Tis our only hope."

"She will not help us, I am sure," answered Madoc. "Mother is very angry with me. Perhaps, you would be the better of the choices to carry out the task."

"She is not happy with me either," William reminded him. "And I need to start on the gown immediately. Time is running out."

"Don't forget, you now promised my lady-in-waiting a gown as well," Abbey pointed out.

A dark cloud settled over William's face. "What did I do? I am doomed. I have doomed us all."

"Oh, stop it," said Abbey, settling herself atop the bed. "Now, Madoc, if you can't convince your mother to get the cloth from Dion, then just steal it and be done with it."

"Steal it?" Madoc frowned. "I could never steal from my own family."

"Oh, really?" William waved his hand through the air, motioning toward Abbey. "Did you already forget how Abbey got the gown she is wearing?"

"I did not steal it," said Madoc. "You gave it to me."

"Nay. I was tricked into it."

"Enough!" shouted Abbey, getting to her feet and going to the door. "Now, you two have work to do, so stop your bickering and get busy." She opened the door, holding it for the two of them to leave.

"Abbey," said Madoc. "I don't want to leave you. You are not safe with that vile man."

"If you two do what you are supposed to do, then I won't have to worry about that for long. Now, if you'll please go, I need to devise a plan to stall the wedding."

William grumbled and headed out the door but Madoc didn't move.

"I won't leave you," he said stubbornly, pulling her into his arms. He went to kiss her, but Abbey stopped him.

"'Tis not safe," she said, her eyes wandering over to the staircase. "We will have plenty of time for this later. Please, go before you are discovered." With that, she gently pushed Madoc out of the room and closed the door behind him.

CHAPTER 12

*M*adoc knew something wasn't right as soon as he heard the commotion in front of his home. He'd changed out of his disguise and back into his own clothes before coming here. Instead of using the front gate, he'd snuck into town using the hidden hole in the wall covered with vines that he'd discovered years ago. After all, he was a wanted man. Hiding under the hood of his cloak so as not to be seen, Madoc surveyed the crowd of people from two streets away. He crept closer to find out details.

He could see Dion, the master tailor and William's mentor, who must have just returned from his journey. The aging, short man held his hands up to hold back the crowd. They were shouting and he shouted back.

"We want him out of here," yelled one man.

"Our children are no longer safe," added a woman.

"Please," said Dion. "I fear for our safety just like the rest of you, but you cannot blame Madoc for this."

"'Tis his fault your lover is near death," shouted a man. "You should hate him more than the rest of us."

Madoc's heart raced. Something was wrong and it had to do with his mother. He slipped behind the houses and ran until he came upon his back yard. He scurried up the staircase, only to be stopped by the silence of his birds. He wanted to go check them yet, at the same time, he couldn't waste a moment. Instead, he rushed into his home to find his mother.

"Mother?" he called, scanning the room but not seeing her anywhere. "Mother?" he repeated a little louder.

That's when the butcher's wife, Imogen, came out from his mother's bedchamber. Following her was a young woman that Madoc recognized as her daughter, although he couldn't remember her name.

"Do not even come near her," Imogen warned him. "'Tis your fault she is near death."

"What happened?" asked Madoc, ignoring her warning and pushing past her. He entered the room and froze, unable to move. His mother lie atop the bed, bruised, swollen and obviously beaten. Her body was wrapped with cloth bandages to stop the flow of blood. By the stains upon them, he could tell her wounds were many. One cheek was swollen and her face was purple and black from the beating she'd endured.

"God's bones! Who did this to you?" Madoc ran to her side and tried to take her into his arms. Tears filled his eyes. He didn't understand any of this. She stirred, and her eyes fluttered open. The fear and despair he saw within them about broke his heart.

"It was a band of thieves," Imogen's daughter told him.

"They came here looking for you," Imogen added.

"Gruffydd," Madoc ground out, wanting to kill the man.

"They stole what little your mother has, and also saw to

ransacking Dion's store," Imogen snorted, crossing her arms over her bosom.

"Was Dion attacked as well?" he asked.

"Nay," answered her daughter. "He had not yet returned from his trip at the time."

"How did they know where to find me?" asked Madoc. The women didn't know, but it no longer mattered. He would not let Gruffydd and his men get away with this.

"Mother, speak to me. Please."

She tried to open her mouth to speak, but no words came forth.

"She is near death," came a voice at the door to the bedchamber. He looked over his shoulder to see Dion enter the room. Dion nodded to the women and they left. "If I hadn't returned when I did, they might have killed her. With the help of the townspeople, we managed to scare them off."

"How did this happen?" asked Madoc. "Why?"

"They were looking for you, Madoc." The man shook his balding head. "You have endangered the whole town by returning. And now your mother lies dying because you thought to bring that girl here with you."

"This wasn't because of Abbey," said Madoc, wanting to protect her even though she wasn't here. "These men were after me."

"The thieves said you had something of theirs."

Madoc looked down to Abbey's dagger still attached to his waist belt. This is what they wanted. This is what caused all this damage and despair. And it was all his fault.

"I am sorry, Madoc, but you will have to leave," Dion told him in a low voice. "And I cannot allow you back here or in my shop again."

"But William has gone to Shrewsbury Castle by request," Madoc told him. "He is to make a wedding gown for Lady Abigail. I will stay and take care of mother."

"Nay. I have some of the townspeople to help look after her. You have been like a son to me through the years, Madoc, but I cannot allow you to stay. You are endangering the entire town."

"William needs your help," Madoc tried to convince him. "He needs some fine silk to make a wedding gown."

"The thieves have stolen most everything from me. I cannot give you anything. I still have my new shipment secure, but I need what little is left in order to survive."

"Then let me at least say goodbye to my mother."

Dion nodded slightly. Madoc walked over to the bed and took his mother's hand in his. Her eyes were closed but she opened one eye to see him.

"I promise you I will kill them for what they did to you, Mother," Madoc promised her in a hoarse voice. "And no harm will ever come to you again, because I am leaving. Forever."

He kissed her gently atop the head and was heading for the door when she stopped him.

"Madoc," she called. Her voice was naught more than a faint whisper. He turned and came back to her side.

"Aye, Mother. I am here."

"I am so sorry," she said with a tear glistening in her eye.

"Nay, I am the one who is sorry. You have naught for which to apologize."

"I am being punished," she said, so softly that Madoc had to lean over to hear her. "God knows I did wrong to you and I deserve to die."

"What kind of nonsense is this?" he asked. "You have never done anything to me but love me. How can God punish you for that?"

"Your . . . mother was . . . dead," she said, barely able to talk. "Your . . . father was gone and died soon after. I . . . wanted a baby. I am sorry."

"Mother, you make no sense. Are you saying . . . you are not really my mother? I don't understand at all."

Before she had time to explain, Madoc was distracted by Dion's shout from the door.

"Madoc, come quickly. 'Tis your birds!"

Madoc jumped to his feet, leaving his mother and rushing through the back door. He was met by Dion holding a dead pigeon in his hand. Blood was splattered over the bird's feathers.

"Nay," shouted Madoc, anger coursing through him by what he saw.

"'Twas the thieves," explained Dion. "They must have done this as a message to you."

"How many?" he asked, but Dion did not answer. "How many did they kill?" Madoc shouted, needing to know. Dion looked into Madoc's eyes and slowly shook his head.

Madoc took the rungs of the ladder two at a time. He rushed over to his pen and threw open the door. The sight that assaulted his senses was more than he could bear. More than half of his birds lie bloody and dead from Gruffydd's attack. They'd managed to kill off all his breeders and even smash the eggs. They'd also killed most of his flyers. Only one survived. And only about a dozen birds sitting high near the ceiling and flying around frightened were all that he had left.

"I will kill those bastards!" he vowed. "I'll make them pay

for what they did to my mother and my birds. I will kill them all!"

"Control yourself, Madoc," warned Dion. "You are already a fugitive. You don't need to add murder to your list of crimes."

Madoc grabbed a box and started gathering up his dead pigeons. He handled each one reverently and with respect. These were his friends – his children in a way. His mother lie dying in the house and now half his flock was gone as well. Where would it end, he asked himself? How did things get so out of hand? He wished he could change his life and the circumstances in it. But things were this way because of the choices he'd made. This was no one's fault but his own.

Holding the door to the pen open, Dion stepped inside. He shook his head in sorrow, taking the box of pigeons from Madoc. "Go," he said. "I will handle this."

"Nay," Madoc objected.

"Madoc, I can see you have just about lost everything. And though I don't agree with the way you live your life, I care deeply for your mother. I know she would never forgive me if I didn't do something to help you."

"But this is all my fault," said Madoc. "If only I could make things right. I have done an injustice to you and, for this, I am deeply sorry."

"Nay, Madoc. I am sorry for being upset with you. I am an old man, and my life is nearly over. But you have your entire life ahead of you yet. Do not go down the wrong path any longer. There is still time to right your wrongs, but you need to change quickly."

"I no longer know what is wrong or right," he told Dion, looking around the pen and shaking his head in despair.

"Take the new silks I brought back and give them to William," he said. "Only you can help him and the woman you love. Now, go."

"But I have no money. I cannot pay you."

"I will survive." Dion sadly looked down to the dead pigeons in the box.

Madoc's eyes roamed over to the jeweled dagger hanging at his waist. He took it in two hands and held it out in front of him. "Take this," he said. "Sell it. It will make up for your losses."

"Is that what the thieves were looking for?" Dion asked. "If so, I do not want it."

Dion was right, Madoc realized. By leaving the dagger with him, it would only endanger him more. Besides, Abbey would never forgive him. It wasn't his to give away.

"I will repay you," said Madoc. "I promise I will."

"I do not want anything if it comes from your thieving."

Madoc never felt as helpless or worthless as he did at this moment. His life was changing since he'd met Abbey. But he realized it was changing for the worse. And everyone he cared about was getting hurt in the process.

He descended the ladder from the roof, taking the box from Dion so the man could follow. Madoc would help him bury every last one of his birds before he left. He couldn't stop thinking what his mother had said to him. It was something he didn't understand, and he needed to talk to her once more.

Just then, Imogen came out of the house and saw them with the dead birds. "Oh," she said. "I am sorry. Did you want me to give them to my husband? The people of the town are hungry, and the birds would make a good meal."

"You won't be eating these birds," Madoc told her. "I'm sorry, but I just can't allow it."

Imogen nodded, and then looked over to Dion. "Gwyneth is sleeping."

"But I need to speak with her," protested Madoc.

"Nay, she is too weak and needs her rest if she is to heal." Imogen blocked the doorway with her body, having no intention of letting Madoc enter.

"Go downstairs to my shop and take what you need for William," Dion instructed. "I will bury your birds and see to cleaning up the pen."

"I will help you first," he answered.

"Nay. The best way you can help anyone right now is to give William what he needs and leave this town before there is any more trouble. The townspeople do not want you here, and I cannot risk another riot."

Madoc knew he was right. He also knew Imogen was right in saying the townspeople were hungry. Was he being selfish by not allowing his birds to be eaten even though they were already dead? He handed the box to Dion. It hurt him deeply, but he was trying to change, like Dion suggested.

"Do what you wish with the birds," he told the man. "But please, just do not tell me. Sometimes not knowing hurts less than finding out the truth."

He meant that in more ways than one. He no longer knew if he wanted to hear what his mother was trying to tell him. Still, it was about his past, and something he had been trying to find out his entire life. He would be back to see his mother, but not today. First he would deliver the supplies to William and then hunt down Gruffydd and his men and kill for the first time in his life.

CHAPTER 13

*A*bbey paced the floor of her tower room, wondering what was taking Madoc so long. She'd returned from morning mass with Lord Shrewsbury nearly an hour ago. She'd sent Bernadette to see William in his solar, supposedly to talk about the gown he was to make for her. She'd just been trying to get her to leave before Madoc returned.

Abbey had even talked the woman into leaving the door unlocked. If Lord Shrewsbury had known, he never would have let her convince him earlier that she no longer needed a guard at the door. But she'd acted like the ever-obedient wife-to-be this morning, playing into the hands of the ogre only to get him to trust her. She knew Lord Shrewsbury would not be able to climb the stairs to check on her, and promised Bernadette she wouldn't leave the room. But now, she was going to have to break that promise.

Abbey had her hand on the door when it opened from the other side. To her surprise, she saw an old woman standing there. When a hairy arm reached out to touch her on the shoulder, she almost screamed until she heard Madoc's voice.

"'Tis me," he said gently, pushing her back into the room and closing the door behind them. He pulled off a fake crop of long, gray hair and tossed it to the side. Then he opened an old, brown cape and she saw what made up the two bumps at his chest. Tied to him were two bags filled with sand. He removed them and tossed them on the bed.

"You're disguised as an old woman now?" she asked with a laugh.

"The guards were checking all the men coming through the gate. I didn't have a choice." He hurriedly untied the bags and dumped out the contents. To her surprise, they weren't filled with sand at all. He'd managed to collect a white, shiny satin and a gold fabric, too. There was another smaller bag he threw down after untying it from around his stomach. "There is lace and adornments in there."

"You are quite resourceful," Abbey answered with a smile. But Madoc wasn't smiling back. She could see that something was troubling him immensely. His normally bright, green eyes were usually filled with sparkle, life, and excitement. Now, they were sad and clouded over with despair.

"What is it?" she asked him. "What is wrong?"

He looked right at her and she could swear she saw tears in his eyes. She had never seen him look so upset.

"My mother is nearly dead, over half my birds have been killed, and only I am to blame."

"What?" She couldn't believe what she was hearing. "What happened? Who did this to them?"

"'Tis the group of bandits that attacked you on the road. 'Tis a group I once ran with, but not for long at all. They were looking for me. They wanted this." He removed her jeweled dagger from his waist and threw it on the bed. "I regret ever stealing it from them in the first place."

"I am so sorry," she said, pulling him into her arms. He nuzzled his face into her hair and she wished she could make things better for him. "Is your mother going to die?" she asked.

"I don't know," he said. "I am not sure I should even care."

"What do you mean by that?" She pushed away and looked to him for an explanation for his calloused remark.

"I knew she'd been keeping a secret from me my entire life. Tonight, she said something that I don't understand. Something that could change everything."

Abbey pulled him over to the bed and sat, motioning for him to sit next to her. "What did she say?" she asked him.

"She said – she was sorry. And something about my mother being dead and my father being gone and dying soon afterward and that she'd wanted a baby."

"So what does that mean?" Abbey didn't understand either.

"I don't know. Not exactly. But I know who does. Do you know where William is right now?"

"He should be in his solar," she said. "But we will be going to the great hall to dine soon. If you want to talk with him, you had better hurry."

Madoc stood up and started shoving the fabric back into the bags. "I am so sorry, Abbey, for any trouble I have caused you."

"What are you talking about?"

"I wish that I could help you, but you will be better off without me." He gathered up all the things needed for William, and headed to the door.

Something was amiss and that fact was verified when she noticed that he'd left her dagger on the bed.

"Are you leaving me, Madoc?" she asked, but already knew the answer.

"I cannot endanger anyone's life again. Especially not yours." He put the bags down and came back to her and pulled her into his arms. "I love you, Abbey. I really do. If only things could be different between us – but you know they can't. I am naught but a thief in the night, just like you said. You deserve someone better. Much better than me." He kissed her then. But before she could even respond, he was heading back to the door.

"Where will you go?" she asked. "What will you do?"

"First, I will hear the truth from William about the secret they are keeping from me. Then I have a band of thieves to hunt down and kill, one by one."

"Nay," she cried. "Madoc, you are not a murderer."

"I will be, soon."

"But 'tis not like you. You don't even have a weapon. I doubt that you even know how to use one."

He perused her with sad eyes, picking up the bags and throwing them over his back.

"Mayhap I should just kill with my bare hands then. Goodbye, Abbey. I am sorry."

Abbey followed him down the winding staircase, furious that he was acting this way. What happened back in town had affected him so much that he was contemplating murder. She couldn't let him do it. She knew he was a thief, but his anger was going to turn him into something he would regret for the rest of his life.

"Madoc, please wait. I need to talk to you." Abbey rushed

after him, but when he reached the bottom of the stairs, he made a beeline toward William's chamber.

"There is naught to talk about," he said. "I have made up my mind."

He threw open the door to William's room and stopped so abruptly that she ran right into the back of him. When she looked around his shoulder, she saw why. There on the bed, naked and in the throes of heated passion, were William and Bernadette.

"God's eyes," he growled under his breath. He dropped the bags onto the floor. Abbey pushed past him, and William and Bernadette looked up in surprise.

"My lady," cried Bernadette, jumping to her feet, holding a coverlet in front of her to shield her naked body from their eyes.

"Madoc," said William, following suit.

"What the hell are you doing?" asked Madoc. Anger and disappointment resounded in his voice. "'Tis not bad enough I almost get everyone killed, but now you are going to add to it as well. I cannot stay here a moment longer."

He turned on his heel and left. Abbey watched him disappear, only hoping this goodbye was not forever.

* * *

MADOC RODE HARD through the woods, traveling the rest of the day and not even stopping until darkness covered the land. He had let the cool breeze blow through his hair, hoping it would take with it all his worries and troubles.

He no longer knew right from wrong. He had endangered the people he cared about and brought upon the death of over half his flock in Shrewsbury. None of this should have ever happened. A new life was what he wanted, now more than ever. Madoc wasn't sure what to do, but something had to change soon.

After stopping his horse near a stream, Madoc dismounted. He would stay here for the night and continue looking for Gruffydd and his men come morning. After taking care of his horse, he gathered wood and made a fire. The twigs snapped and flames shot up, warming him and giving him a false sense of comfort and security.

He dug through his travel bags, looking for food. Having left in such a hurry, he hadn't had time to gather supplies. There was naught in the bag but a stale hunk of bread left over from his travels with Abbey. He also found the guard's clothes and cape he had borrowed – or stolen. They would be used tonight as a ground covering and coverlet when he slept.

Thankfully, there was a sheep's bladder half-full of water in the bag. He gripped it in one hand and sat down by the fire.

"Naught better than what I had in the dungeon," he remarked aloud, shaking his head at the stale bread and old water.

How had his life turned so sour so fast? He had been happy with Abbey. She made him feel alive. With her, he felt excitement and a will to change. He had almost believed they could have a life together and someday raise a family. Madoc wanted naught more than to be married to a woman he loved. Hopefully, he'd have several children he could raise and protect, and be able to teach the ways of life.

Who was he fooling? What could he offer a child, let alone a wife? He had no skills to teach a son. Thieving, he was good at, as well as wearing disguises and pretending he was someone he wasn't. But that was something he would never want to teach any child. Shame and embarrassment of his past plagued him and he knew he could not change it at all.

Why couldn't he be admirable? If only he had the title and skills of someone like Lord Corbett Blake. He wished he was a knight or that he had a reputation for being a savage warrior, like the Highlander, Storm MacKeefe. But he was neither. He had been raised by a woman and not a man who could teach him these things. His mother had raised two boys on her own. She did what she had to do in order to survive. Or did she? He suddenly wondered.

What did his mother mean when she said she was sorry and that his parents were dead? Who were his parents and how did she come to raise him as her own? And what, in Heaven's name, did she mean when she said she wanted a baby?

Madoc had meant to shake the truth from William but once he saw him coupling with a lady from the castle, he realized his brother was no better than him. What they had done would only cause trouble and, perhaps, more deaths. Madoc had been so angry with William that he'd just had to leave before he hurt someone else.

Now, the idea of trying to go back and talk to his mother filled his head. 'Twas what he really needed to do. But Dion told him he was no longer welcome in town. And his mother, for all he knew, could already be dead. Nay, he couldn't endanger anyone again by his presence.

It didn't matter because, deep down, he was almost afraid to hear the truth from his mother. The way his luck was running, he would find out he was the bastard son of an infamous murderer or the child of a whore. He couldn't fathom

151

his life being any worse than it already was. Right now, his mind was too confused and consumed with revenge to even care.

His jaw tired from trying to gnaw the hard bread. With a flick of his wrist, he threw it into the fire and took the last swig of clouded water. He then settled atop the cape that served as his bed. Exhausted physically, emotionally, and mentally, he fell into a deep slumber instantly. He could only hope his dreams that night would be of a much better life.

* * *

ABBEY HAD BEEN SO shocked at seeing Bernadette and William together that she had turned and left the room right after Madoc. But instead of going back to her tower room, she made her way to the dungeon to try to see her brother.

Her heart already ached for Madoc. She could not imagine what emotions controlled him at a time like this. He felt responsible for the near death of his mother and the deaths of his birds, but she thought he was being harsh with himself. In her heart, she knew Madoc would never want for anything but good to come to those he cared about. She also knew he was leaving because he felt he would only bring her doom as well.

What he didn't understand was that she needed him now more than ever. In two days' time, she would be married to a man she didn't love. Never would she willingly be the wife of a man she feared and loathed. And now, her only thought was that she needed to find a way to help her brother escape. Together, they could flee the walls of Shrewsbury Castle and never look back.

Abbey approached the dungeon, blocked by a guard who shook his head as she came to his side.

"No ladies are allowed in the dungeon," he told her.

"But I am the lady of the castle," she answered. "Surely, you don't mean me."

"Lord Shrewsbury's orders were not to let you near your brother, Lady Abigail. I cannot let you pass."

An old woman approached, bringing food and ale for the prisoners. The guard unlocked the iron door that led to the cells and she entered the dungeon.

"Why do you let her pass?" she asked. "Is she not a woman also?"

"She is naught but an old serving wench, so she doesn't matter. My lord refuses to send in the comely girls, for fear the prisoners would enjoy it too much."

That gave her an idea, and she headed back up to the great hall. The midday meal was being served and if she wasn't there, her presence would be missed. She didn't want to arouse any suspicion amongst Lord Shrewsbury and his men because, if so, they might discover that she was planning an escape.

She sauntered into the great hall. Bernadette ran up to greet her.

"My lady," she said frantically but in a hushed whisper. "I beg you not to mention my time with William to Lord Shrewsbury. He would beat me for my behavior."

"Of course not," she said, laying a hand on the woman's shoulder. "You keep my secrets and I will keep yours."

"Aye, my lady. Of course. I understand and appreciate your generous kindness."

"Tell me, when do the guards at the dungeon change shifts?"

"I believe right after the meal, my lady. But why do you ask?"

"I need you to help me disappear from Lord Shrewsbury's sight with a good reason, as soon as the meal is finished."

"But . . . the lord has entertainment planned and will expect you to be at his side."

"Then we will have to think of a good excuse."

Before they could continue, Lord Shrewsbury hobbled over to them. He held out his arm, wanting to escort Abigail to the table.

"What took you so long?" he snapped. "I expect my wife to be on time for the meals and not to make me wait."

"Of course, my lord," she said, laying her hand atop his arm, letting him escort her to the dais.

"I have yet to talk to that clumsy tailor," he told her. "I want to know how the plans are progressing for your wedding gown."

"Well, having to secure his own satin put him at a disadvantage," she told him. "Had you supplied the materials, I am sure, by now, the dress would be finished." She knew this would roil him, and also that he was too greedy to want to part with any of his own money to see to the chore. "As soon as I take over the tallies, I will make sure he is paid dearly for what he has had to endure."

"You will do no such thing. My tallies will not be put into your hands. I have my steward to do that." He brought her to the dais and bowed slightly, giving the signal for the rest of the inhabitants to be seated and for the meal to begin.

"No disrespect intended, but as lady of the castle I am

expected to run your household in your absence. I am sure you would want me to be able to handle any situation."

"You do not need to worry about your duties until after you are my wife." He held out his hands to the ewerer who washed them. She did the same when the young lad approached her.

"I think 'tis important that, as your wife, I start handling your estate as is proper, right away. Therefore, I require to no longer be locked in my chamber no better than one of your prisoners in the dungeon. I will roam the castle freely."

"Do not tell me what to do or I will beat you," he snarled, taking a leg of meat and ripping the meat off the bone with his teeth.

"Being married is quite different than you are used to, I would dare to say."

"You would be better served to keep your mouth shut and only speak when I instruct you to."

Abbey nibbled at her food, knowing she was treading in deep waters. Still, she had to take the chance, as she no longer had Madoc to help her.

When the dinner was almost finished, she looked around for Bernadette to help her leave the lord's side. She spotted her at the back of the room, head down speaking with William who sat at a table far from Lord Shrewsbury.

"Come, Wife," said Shrewsbury, wiping his mouth on his sleeve. "I will sample what you have to offer before the wedding to see if I like what I am promised."

Abbey quickly scanned the crowd, but Bernadette was not paying attention to her. Her heart raced in her chest knowing Shrewsbury meant to take her to his bed.

"But as your bride-to-be I am to remain a virgin until our wedding night."

"No one but me is going to know the difference. Now, I said let's go!"

When she didn't stand when he did, he grabbed her arm and yanked her to her feet. That caught the attention of most of the people in the room. Thankfully, Bernadette finally looked up.

He hauled her out into the corridor. When she pulled away from him, he looked at her with eyes blazing.

"Do not fight me, wench! I order you to come with me."

"Nay," she said, pulling her arm from his grasp. "This is not what is expected of a lady in my position."

His fist lashed out at her face and she was not as lucky this time to escape the whole blow. She turned her head quickly but his hard knuckles still smashed into her eye. She fell to the ground and he kicked her then, in what she knew was his way of showing he was superior. She curled up into a ball awaiting his next blow. Pain shot through her side and her eye throbbed as it already started to swell.

"My lady!" screamed Bernadette. She ran to Abbey and dropped to her knees to protect her. Several of the lord's knights ran up behind her, followed by William.

The ogre probably would have hit her again, as well as hit Bernadette, had his knights not stopped him. He pushed them away from him and straightened his clothes, seeing naught wrong with hitting a woman. It was certainly not the chivalric way of a seasoned knight.

"Get her out of my sight!" he screamed. "And someone get me a tankard of ale." He went back to the great hall with his men following. One knight stayed behind to help her.

"My lady, my name is Sir Denzil," the knight said, helping her and Bernadette to stand. "I apologize for the crude acts of Lord Shrewsbury. If there is anything I can do to assist you, please let me know."

"Thank you," said Abbey, her voice shaky. Her eye throbbed and she felt like her rib was cracked. "If you'll just send the healer to my chamber, I am certain Lady Bernadette and William can help me up the tower stairs."

"Of course, my lady," he said with a bow and hurried away to carry out her orders.

"Lady Abigail." William took her arm. "I am so sorry."

She made her way up the tower stairs with Bernadette and William helping her. She longed for Madoc at her side right now. But she knew if he'd seen what Lord Shrewsbury had done to her, his anger would cause him to strike back and, no doubt, land him in the dungeon.

"I know you said you wanted an excuse to leave the great hall early," said Bernadette. "But my lady, this is so extreme." She opened the door and they all entered. They helped Abbey over to the bed.

"Believe me, Bernadette, 'twas not what I had in mind."

"Where is Madoc?" William helped settle her on the bed. "He should be here by now."

"He is not returning." Abbey supplied the information.

"What?" asked William, not able to believe her words. "That makes no sense."

"A band of thieves robbed your home, William. They were looking for Madoc. They not only killed over half of Madoc's birds, but they beat your poor mother and left her nearly dead."

"Nay!" he shouted, his eyes wide. "I must go to her at once."

There was a knock at the door. When Bernadette opened it, an old woman stood there – the castle's healer.

"Come in," said Bernadette. The woman nodded and made her way over to Abbey. She spoke little and tended to Abbey's wounds. William paced the floor, waiting for her to leave so they could finish their conversation.

Just as the woman was getting ready to leave, Abbey had an idea.

"Leave the bag of herbs," she told her. "And your cape, also."

"My lady?" the healer asked in bewilderment.

"Lady Bernadette will see that you are compensated," she instructed.

"Of course, my lady," Bernadette said with a nod of her head. She led the old woman from the room, leaving William alone with Abbey.

"Why did you want her cape and herbs?" asked William.

"I am going to use them to get into the dungeon to see my brother," she explained.

"Nay, Abbey," he told her. "'Tis too dangerous. I am sure Madoc would not like it."

"Madoc is not coming back. I need to do whatever I can to save my brother, Garrett, and help him escape before I end up married to that violent man." She touched her eye and could feel the raised welt. She was glad Madoc would not see her in this condition. She was sure she looked hideous.

"Why would you say such a thing?" William asked her. "Madoc loves you. That is the whole reason I am here."

"I am sorry for your involvement," she told him. "And you and Bernadette will need to be careful, lest Lord Shrewsbury catches you in each other's arms. 'Twould be the end of both of you."

"I never meant to do it," he explained. "It just . . . happened. But I really do care for Lady Bernadette." He looked to the ground.

"I understand," she said. "'Twas the same for me and Madoc."

"Abbey, why did he leave? Please tell me."

"I do believe he felt he was to blame for all of the bad things that have happened. He came here to confront you – about something his mother told him of his parents being dead and she wanting a baby."

"She finally told him?" William's eyes looked hopeful.

Abbey straightened up in bed, the pain still shooting through her.

"William, is there something you know that you haven't told your brother about his past? If so, please tell me."

William paced the floor but finally settled himself atop a chair next to the bed. "Nay, I must remain silent. I promised Mother. If anyone knew the secret, it would be the end for us."

"What do you mean, William? Please tell me."

He lowered his face into his hands and let out a deep sigh. "I cannot," he said.

"You cannot or will not?" she asked curiously. "If you know something about Madoc's past, then you need to tell him."

Before he could respond, Bernadette rushed into the room. "William, Lord Shrewsbury is on his way to your chamber to see how the gown is progressing."

"What?" He jumped to his feet. "But I've yet to cut the material and have not even started to sew."

"He is furious," she told him. "He said he is going to lock you into the room until it is completed."

"Nay. My mother is dying. I need to go to her." William looked over to Abbey and then back to Bernadette.

Abbey's eye throbbed and she felt as if someone had thrust a dagger into her heart. She needed Madoc desperately. They all did. If something did not happen to change things soon, they would all be doomed forever.

CHAPTER 14

*M*adoc rode up the hill in Brynmawr to his hut of wattle and daub. He was greeted by Owein, waving a hand in the air.

"Welcome back," shouted Owein, smiling and happy to see him. "I have taken care of everything in yer absence. Me and my son, Hadyn, that is."

"My many thanks," said Madoc, dismounting and heading straight for the pen. It was good to see his birds here were alive and well. He couldn't get the awful massacre out of his mind from the pen in Shrewsbury.

"Will ye be staying this time?" asked Owein. "And what about the girl? Where is she?"

Madoc stopped in his tracks, feeling the emptiness in his heart at this question. "I am not sure how long I'll be staying," he told the man. "And the girl – the girl is . . . going to marry Lord Shrewsbury on the morrow."

"What?" asked Owein, following him into the pen. The birds flew around Madoc, happy to see him. "I thought ye two were together. Why is she marrying someone else? I don't understand."

Neither did Madoc. He'd thought he had his whole life figured out until Abbey came into it and rocked the ship upon the waters. He still wanted her as his wife. He always would. He was used to taking whatever he wanted, having done it his entire life. Leaving Abbey behind was the hardest thing he had ever done.

Madoc scattered seed for his birds. Homer flew right over to him and landed on his shoulder. He took her in two hands and looked her in the eye. She stared back with her mismatched eyes. One was black and the other a cross of orange and red. He found himself thinking it reminded him of the differences between Abbey and himself. Here, he felt almost as if he were home. However, something wasn't quite right, but he couldn't place it.

The faint chirps from the breeding pen called to him so Madoc put down Homer to investigate. As soon as he approached, he knew the squabs were pushing their way out of the eggs. He saw a fat beak sticking out from the shell of one, and an eye looking out of another. They made small squeaking sounds since they could not yet coo.

"Welcome to the world, little squeakers," he said, smiling to know that while his others died, these would live.

"So, are ye still planning on racing yer pigeons for the prize money?" asked Owein.

Madoc felt a sadness envelop him, thinking of the valuable birds he'd lost.

"I lost most of my flyers," Madoc explained. "The same thieves that roughed you up came looking for me there. They not only robbed us, but killed over half my flock and almost killed my mother."

"I am so sorry, Madoc. I had no idea. How did they know where to find ye?"

"I am not sure. But I could have saved the flyers, had I not been so distracted. I should have released them first thing upon my return. They were all killed but one. And, of course, Homer is safe," he explained nodding toward his favorite bird. "Also, the messenger I left with you who will fly to her home in Shrewsbury if needed. I am only glad I'd yet to take Homer to Shrewsbury because that saved her life. But I will collect her and take her there soon in anticipation of the upcoming race."

"So ye are still going to race with only two birds to fly from Shrewsbury to here?"

"I have no choice. Because of me, Dion has lost nearly everything he owns. I need that prize money to pay back my debt. I have been very selfish in my choices, Owein. I need to make amends to the people I hurt, but I am not sure how."

"I know ye, Madoc. Ye will make sure those ye care about are safe. Ye won't let anyone hurt the ones ye love."

Madoc didn't answer as he stared at the chicks emerging from the eggs. They were so strong and determined, just like Abbey. But these chicks had their parents. Abbey had no one looking after her now. She was all alone. Owein was right when he said Madoc always looked after those he loved. So why in Heaven's name had he left Abbey alone with that wolf, Lord Shrewsbury?

Madoc no longer knew who or what he was. But one thing he did know was that he had just abandoned the people he cared about the most. He only hoped his decision would not cost them their lives.

* * *

ABBEY MADE her way down to the dungeon slowly. The pain in her side hurt like the devil, and she could barely see out of her swollen eye. She'd donned the fake crop of hair that Madoc had left in her room. It smelled like horse's hair, and she was sure the gray within it was from flour or some kind of powder.

She wore the cape that she'd instructed the healer to leave and, in her hand, she held the bag of healing herbs. Hidden under the folds of her gown, she had attached her jeweled dagger that Madoc had thrown on the bed in anger.

"Who goes there?" called a voice in the dark.

Abbey cocked her head to use her good eye. In the torch-light, she could see the dungeon guard with his hand on the hilt of his sword.

"'Tis me, the healer," she said, trying to make her voice sound old, the way Madoc had done. "I am here to check the prisoners."

The guard looked at her quizzically as if he didn't believe her. But when she walked bent over and limping from her bout with Shrewsbury, he seemed to consider she really was the old healer after all. Still, he did not let her pass.

"Show me your face, old woman," the guard said.

She kept herself bent over and stared up at him with one purple and black, bruised and swollen eye. He grimaced as if repulsed and looked away.

"Give me your bag so I can make sure you are not

sneaking in weapons."

She handed over the bag of herbal creams and cloth bandages and he finally seemed convinced.

"All right," he said, shoving the bag back into her hands. "But you have ten minutes, no more."

She followed him in through the door, and quickly looked around for her brother. There were many men in the dungeon. They moaned and wailed as she entered. The putrid smell about gagged her, and she almost jumped in surprise as a rat ran right over her feet.

"I am being sent to patch the one called Garrett," she said, hoping the guard would not become suspicious. "I need you to take me to him."

"Aye, he has been in need of mending for some time now. I am surprised Lord Shrewsbury wants to help him, since he is going to hang him right after the wedding."

"What?" She spoke in her own voice, and then caught herself. "What do you mean? I thought he was to be set free in exchange for the hand of the girl in marriage."

"Since when does Lord Shrewsbury care about the deals he makes? I heard he even beat his bride-to-be today."

"Aye," she said, having the bruises and pain to prove it.

"Just hurry," he said. "I have known Lord Shrewsbury to change his mind rapidly. It would not be unlike him to follow you down here and order you to leave before you can mend the man."

He stopped in front of a cell and put the iron key into the lock. The lock creaked as he turned the key, and the door swung open.

She froze when she saw the crumpled body of her brother huddled against the far wall of the cell. He looked up slowly.

She almost gasped at the sight of the welts and bruises that encompassed his body.

His face was covered with dirt and his hair hung scraggly and matted nearly down to his waist. It looked like they had not even washed him or fed him much in the year he'd been locked away. Her heart went out to him and she cursed herself for her own selfishness in trying to escape coming here at all. Had she known he was in this condition, she would have come willingly in order to spare him. But then again, as she just found out, her alliance here would do nothing to help him.

The guard stood behind her as she entered, planning on watching her the entire time. She would never be able to speak to her brother freely if he didn't leave.

"I need water to cleanse the wounds," she told him. "Can you get some for me?"

The guard hesitated, but then agreed. "I do not think he has the strength to hurt you but, either way, I will lock you in with him so he doesn't try to escape."

The guard locked the cell door behind her and a sickening feeling lodged in her chest as if she'd be trapped there forever. When he left to get water, she hurried to her brother and took him into her arms.

"Garrett," she whispered. "'Tis your sister, Abigail."

He slowly looked up to her and she could see death in the darkness of his eyes. No light or sparkle shone within like she'd seen from Madoc's eyes when she'd first met him.

"Ab . . . Abi . . . gail?" he said, his lips caked and dry, and barely moving.

"I am here to help you," she said, pulling out the herbal creams and bandages. She didn't know where to start. His body was so battered and broken that she wanted to cry. "Who did this to you?" she asked. "Was it Shrewsbury?"

"Aye," came a voice from outside the cell door behind her. "'Twas me, my Lady Abigail."

She stood up and spun around to see Lord Shrewsbury standing outside the cell door. The guard was right behind him.

"Lord Shrewsbury," she said in her own voice, since he already knew her ploy. "I only wanted to see my brother."

"And so you have," he told her. "And now you will stay right there where I know you will not escape until we are married on the morrow."

Abbey cursed under her breath. This was not at all how she had planned things. And just when she didn't think things could get worse, they did. Oh, how she wished Madoc were here to save her.

"I cannot marry you because I will not have a gown in time," she told him.

"Well, if the tailor does not finish in time, then I will have to kill him," stated Shrewsbury.

"You can't do that," she cried. "You cannot expect him to finish a gown in a day. That's preposterous."

"Well, he seemed to have no trouble finishing your first gown in a day, now did he?"

She couldn't say anything to that. If she did, then he would be sure to kill William for the deception he and Madoc pulled upon him. She had to think of an excuse quickly.

"Well, my body is bruised and swollen. You won't want to show me like that."

"I no longer care. 'Twill be a reminder to the rest of the castle of what I can do if they disobey me. And if the gown is not finished in time, then after I kill the tailor, you can stand before the entire castle and recite your vows naked!"

She'd obviously managed to make the man angry again. And this time, she did not see a way out of the situation. He turned to leave, and the guard came to the cell door. When he was sure Lord Shrewsbury could not hear, he spoke.

"I am sorry, Lady Abigail, as are many of the lord's men. But we must obey him."

"Did you inform him of my whereabouts?" she asked.

"Nay," the man answered. "He said he saw you coming down the tower stairs. He'd also seen the healer leaving just before that."

The guard handed her a sheep's bladder of water in between the bars. Then, after scanning the area with a quick sweep of his eyes, he pulled out a loaf of bread from under his cloak and handed her that as well.

"Thank you," said Abbey, feeling like it was the last meal she or her brother would ever have. "But why do you help us?"

"I have worked at the castle for many years, my lady. I was once loyal to the late Lord Shrewsbury, and that is why he granted me this position. But I am not proud to say I deceived a young co-worker years ago. I revealed to my lord that he had stolen from his mews. The man ended up imprisoned because of me. I will do whatever I can to help prisoners now to make up for the friendship I lost that day."

Abbey had a feeling this man had something to do with Madoc's past. The story sounded very similar to the one Madoc told her.

"What is your name?" she asked.

"'Tis better if you do not know. I don't want it known to Lord Shrewsbury that I helped you."

As soon as he walked away, Abbey ran to her brother. She started by giving him the vessel of water. His hands came up slowly, shaking, trying to hold it. She then started to tend to his wounds. When she pulled his tunic to the side, she saw the lashes on his back.

"Good God in Heaven," she exclaimed. "The wretched man has whipped you!"

"Abbey," Garrett said slowly as she tended to his wounds. "You need to get out of here. Do not worry . . . about me."

"I would never leave you here with that monster. We will find a way to escape together."

When she finished wrapping his wounds, she broke off a piece of bread and gave it to him. He shoved it into his mouth eagerly. She followed it with more water, wondering when he'd last been fed.

"Lord Shrewsbury plans on hanging you right after the wedding," she told him. "But don't worry, I will get us out of here before then." She patted the dagger hidden in her clothing, wondering if she were going to have to murder someone in order to escape. So much hatred for the man flowed through her blood for what he did to her brother. Plus, he beat her, as well, so she had no qualms about killing the Lord of Shrewsbury if it came to that.

Then she thought of Madoc and how she had told him he would be naught but a murderer if he killed the ones who hurt his mother and his birds. Now, she understood how he felt. Her heart ached and she wished she could have one last chance to see him again to tell him she understood him and accepted any decision he made. But it was too late now. Because by the morrow, she would be married to a murderer and her brother would be dead by her vile husband's hand.

* * *

MADOC RODE like the devil through the woods, trying to reach the castle before Abbey was married. He'd had time to think things over and it was nice to have Owein knocking some sense into his brain. He realized he was running from his troubles instead of confronting them. Madoc had never run from anything in his life and wasn't about to start now.

He had left in such a hurry that he did not have time to take Homer back to Shrewsbury with him. But he decided Homer was safer where she was for now.

Madoc decided that his past and his mother's secret no longer mattered. He had to live for the day, not in the past or for the future. True, he was a thief. But while he was not proud of it, he still had skills. He would use his skill to steal not only Abbey, but also her brother right out from under Shrewsbury's nose. He only hoped he'd get there in time to devise a plan before 'twas too late.

He would travel all night if need be, just to make it there in time to save Abbey from marrying Shrewsbury on the morrow.

* * *

WILLIAM FRANTICALLY SEWED the wedding gown, knowing 'twas far from his best work. Still, there was no way he would be done in time for the wedding on the morrow. Lord Shrewsbury had not only posted a guard at his door, but told him if it wasn't done in time he would be executed.

His hands shook. Why had he let Madoc talk him into this? And what, he wondered, had happened to his mother?

For all he knew, she could be dead while he was trapped here, unable to help her.

There was a slight knock at the door and Bernadette entered. She had a worried look upon her face.

"Lady Bernadette," said William, rising to meet her. "What are you doing here? Shouldn't you be with Abbey?"

"Oh, William, 'tis awful. Abbey is locked in the dungeon with her brother. Lord Shrewsbury plans on keeping her there until the wedding."

"Nay, tell me this isn't so."

"And I heard from the guard that the command has been given to send for the executioner. Her brother is to die. Lord Shrewsbury has no intention of keeping his promise of setting him free."

"This is awful," said William, pacing the floor, trying to think. "I don't know what to do. I only wish Madoc were here. As it is, I will never finish sewing in time, and I, too, will be executed because of it."

"That, I can help you with," she said with a slight smile. "Give me some pieces to be sewn. I will take them up to the lady's solar. My ladies know how to stitch with expertise. We will all help you to finish in time."

William's body stopped shaking and a smile of relief crossed his face. "You are wonderful, Lady Bernadette. Thank you so much."

"Do not thank me until we know for certain Lady Abigail is safe. I have no idea how we are going to help her and her brother."

CHAPTER 15

*A*bbey had spent the worst night of her life in the dungeon. Rats kept nibbling at her feet and she was thankful to have her dagger to poke at them to keep them away. Her brother, Garrett, had barely stirred throughout the night and that concerned her. If she hadn't tended to his wounds and given him bread and water, he wouldn't have made it until the morning. It was cold and damp, and while she was clothed, her brother's body was only covered in torn, thin clothes. She'd removed her cape and wrapped it around him, as well as taken the horsehair disguise from her head and used it to keep him warm.

It was dark in the dungeon and she had no real idea if 'twas morning. She could only guess 'twas morning, because she thought she'd heard the guards changing watch. The door to the main dungeon squeaked open and she could hear heels clicking against the stone floor as several people came forward.

"So how did my little bride sleep last night?" Lord Shrewsbury stood at the cell door. He was not at all the person she wanted to see.

"I did not sleep," she retorted. "But I would welcome sleeping in the dungeon any time over sleeping with you."

She'd angered him again, and he ordered the guard to open the cell door. The guard was the man who'd helped her last night. Hopefully, he would do something to help her again. She thought Shrewsbury meant to release her, but then she realized her mistake when she saw the hooded executioner walk up behind him.

"I called for the executioner, and he arrived early. Therefore, I see no sense waiting to kill your brother. We will do it anon, before the wedding instead of afterward. That way, I can focus all my attention on our celebration and not worry that you will try to help him again."

"Nay!" she screamed, and ran to protect her brother. He lay on the floor, not moving. Then, when the guard opened the door, Lord Shrewsbury stepped in and reached out to grab her.

She quickly ripped the hidden dagger from under her clothes and lashed out at Lord Shrewsbury. He cursed when she nicked his arm. That only made him furious. He lashed out and grabbed her hand that still held the dagger. He squeezed so hard that she felt the blood flowing to her hand stop and her fingers become numb.

"I will let you see what it feels like to be scratched by a dagger now," the man growled.

"Lord Shrewsbury," said the executioner in a deep voice. "I have many other executions today and need to move this along quickly."

Shrewsbury glared at Abbey. She wasn't sure if she should thank the executioner or hate him right now.

"Of course," her husband-to-be snarled. "Let us move this along then."

The executioner stepped forward and took the dagger from Abbey. "If you'll allow me, my lord. I will hold on to this before the little lady tries another attempt on your life."

Abbey hadn't been paying much attention to the executioner. But when he took her dagger, his hand lingered while, at the same time, Lord Shrewsbury pulled his away. The executioner's touch was gentle, not what she expected from a man who killed people for a living. Then, she suddenly recognized the disguised voice, and quickly looked up to see his face.

He raised his chin, and she could see his eyes glistening in the light of the dungeon torch. Green. Bright green! Her heart leaped as she realized it was Madoc beneath the disguise.

He pursed his lips into a shhhh, to warn her to keep his identity a secret. Then he released his hand from hers, fastening her dagger to his waist.

"Get the prisoner," Shrewsbury ordered his guard. "Executioner, help him as I am not sure the man can walk."

MADOC FELT the anger pushing through him at the way Shrewsbury was handling Abbey. He almost cried out when she'd raised her face to look at him and he saw the bruises on her body and her swollen eye. He had no doubt in his mind now that he'd done the right thing in returning. Abbey deserved so much better than this. And though he hadn't thought he, himself, was good enough for her, Shrewsbury was lower than the belly of a worm and didn't deserve her.

He helped the guard to lift her brother to his feet. The man was thin and broken. And he had horrible whip marks on his back. A newfound anger burned within Madoc. How could anyone treat a prisoner so cruelly? Especially since this man was allegedly to be set free, using Abbey as the pawn in the bargain.

He had to help him, as well as Abbey. And he had to make certain William was not in danger, as well as make sure his mother was still alive. Why had he ever left here in the first place, doubting himself and doubting his love for Abbey? He wasted so much precious time that he no longer knew if he could accomplish everything in the short amount of time he had left.

He would take the man to the gallows. The structure was already built and waiting for his execution. Abbey left ahead of him, being dragged along behind Shrewsbury. The man was going to force her to watch her brother go to his death. Madoc only hoped his illusion was going to work the way he had planned. Because if it didn't, her brother would not only go to his death, but Madoc would be the one who killed him.

ABBEY FELT relieved that Madoc was back. He would save her brother. But she didn't know why he wasn't causing a distraction or doing something to stop Lord Shrewsbury from completing this heinous deed. Instead, he was playing his part too well as he now led her brother straight to the gallows.

The courtyard was crowded with not only the castle's

occupants, but also the vendors and villeins of Lord Shrews-bury's demesne. Serfs and villagers filled the area as well. It sickened her how everyone flocked to see a good killing. But they would be surprised when Madoc saved Garrett instead.

Madoc took her brother to the edge of the gallows, taking his time arranging the sack over Garret's face that would keep the onlookers from seeing his eyes as they bulged from his head. The kind guard from the dungeon stood in front of her brother, blocking his body from Abbey's view as he helped Madoc prepare for the execution. Why wasn't he helping save him? His story of remorse he'd told her in the dungeon must have all been a lie after all. But it didn't matter. Any moment now, she was sure Madoc would whisk him away to safety. But instead, he tied Garrett's hands in back of his body. It looked like he said something to him as well. Abbey didn't understand what was going on.

"Have a seat, my lady. The front is reserved for us." Lord Shrewsbury settled himself atop one of the benches lined up for viewing. He pulled her down beside him. The next time she looked up, Madoc was leading her limping brother up the stairs of the gallows.

"Nay," she said under her breath as Madoc fastened the noose around Garrett's neck.

"What's the matter?" Shrewsbury laughed. "Haven't you ever seen a hanging before?"

She noticed the wagon of hay that sat next to the gallows. It would be used to take the dead body away from the castle. A horse was attached and it looked a lot like Madoc's horse if she wasn't mistaken. Mayhap, that was part of the plan for the escape.

"Continue with the hanging," called out Shrewsbury, making Abbey jump in her seat.

Madoc secured the noose one last time. In his executioner ways, he slowly made his way to the lever that would be pulled to release the floor from under Garrett's feet.

Her heart beat rapidly in her chest. She had to trust Madoc. But when he pulled the lever and the floor dropped out, her heart dropped in her chest as well. There was a sickening silence as the crowd watched her brother, hands still tied in back of him, go through the hole in the floor. His body dangled, swinging from the end of the rope. His hooded head fell forward, and his feet danced on the air below him.

"Nay!" she screamed and jumped to her feet. "Garrett," she cried, not able to believe her brother was dead.

Some of the crowd cheered and others mumbled their disapproval of this act. Then Lord Shrewsbury, laughing, got to his feet and grabbed on to her elbow.

"Well, the entertainment is over and now we can prepare for our wedding." He looked over to the guard standing near Madoc. "Help the executioner get the body in the wagon and tell him to take it anywhere as long as 'tis out of my sight."

"How could you?" she spat, beating her fists against Shrewsbury's chest. "You promised my father you would release my brother and, instead, you have taken his life." Tears streamed from her eyes, and her entire body shook in rage.

"'Twas not me who took your brother's life, my dear." He motioned with his head toward Madoc as they headed away. "Right there is the man who pulled the lever that ended your brother's time upon this earth."

She looked at Madoc then, who seemed to be watching their every move. He took her dagger from his side and in one swipe, cut her brother's noose. Garret's body fell onto the straw of the wagon below.

"How could you?" she whispered, now hating Madoc just as much as Lord Shrewsbury. While she thought he had returned to help her, she knew now her trust in him had been misplaced. She could never again even look at the man who killed her brother.

MADOC COULD SEE the look on Abbey's face, and it pained him not to be able to tell her about his plan. The guard helped him throw Garrett's body into the back of the wagon. With his executioner's hood still hiding his face, Madoc tore out of there like a bat escaping hell.

He waited until he was out of sight of the castle guards, pulling the wagon into the woods before he stopped. He then rushed to the back of the wagon, using Abbey's dagger to cut the ropes from Garrett's hands. He helped him remove the burlap sack covering his head, and sat him up, leaning against the side of the wagon.

"Are you all right?" he asked, removing the hook attached to the man's back by means of a harness around his shoulders under his clothes. Madoc was only glad that one of Shrewsbury's dungeon guards had kept his secret and even helped him apply the harness. The guard knew the real executioner well. He knew that the man traveled far to get here and would not truly arrive for yet another day. He knew at once Madoc was not the executioner, but kept his secret, not agreeing with Shrewsbury's decision to go back on his word and kill Garrett instead. The man said he owed it to Madoc, but it made no sense to him. Still, he was happy his plan worked after all and that Abbey's brother had not perished.

Garrett breathed heavily, as he squinted in the light of the bright sun. Madoc was sure it stung his eyes as well as the fair white skin upon his body. He remembered Abbey saying he had been imprisoned for nearly a year now. 'Twas amazing the man still lived. By the look of the welts and whip marks on his body, he had not been treated well.

"I thank you – for my life." Garrett tried to smile, but winced. His lips were cracked and bleeding. Madoc knew he had to be in a lot of pain.

"I am only glad my illusion worked," Madoc told him. "I was not at all sure 'twould hold." He removed the device from around the man and threw it out of the wagon. It landed on the ground with a clunk.

"Who are you?" asked Garrett. "And why would you risk your life to save me?"

"My name is Madoc ap Powell. I am . . . I am a friend of Abbey's."

"I was surprised to see my sister," said Garrett, rubbing his wrists and then his neck. "'Twas good to see her again, although I want to kill Shrewsbury for what he did to her."

"Your father traded her in marriage for your life," Madoc explained.

He winced again in pain. "Had I known, I would never have let her do it."

"They are to be married this afternoon but I mean to stop it." Madoc walked to the front of the wagon, and settled himself atop the seat. "I am going to leave you at St. Alkmund's for now. You have sanctuary there as long as you don't foolishly leave, as your sister did."

He grabbed the reins of the horse and started away, hearing Garrett's weak voice from the back of the wagon. "You love her, don't you? I can see it in your eyes."

"Aye," he admitted. "That I do. But right now, she most likely hates me more than anyone, since she thinks you are dead and that I was the one to do it."

CHAPTER 16

*A*bbey stumbled along behind Shrewsbury as he pulled her into the castle and to William's door. He stopped out front, giving a nod to his guards. Without knocking, he burst into the room.

William sat at his table used for sewing, while Bernadette handed him the scissors. He jumped to his feet when he saw them. Bernadette acknowledged him with a slight curtsey.

"Let me see the gown, tailor. And if 'tis not complete, you will be the next to go to the gallows." Shrewsbury shoved Abbey forward. Bernadette reached out and cradled her in her arms.

Abbey had her eyes closed tight and did not dare open them. She knew William was far from being done in sewing the wedding gown, and she could not sit through another execution. Her body still shook and her mind was numb after seeing her brother die on the gallows.

"Splendid," said Shrewsbury with a tone of admiration to his voice. "You do fine work, tailor."

Abbey wiped tears from her eyes and bravely opened

them. There stood William, holding the gown up in front of him. It was finished, and not bad for the short amount of time he'd had to construct it.

A square neckline trimmed in lace gave way to a cream-colored satin bodice that flowed down into a full skirt. The sleeves were full, trimmed in gold and reached all the way down to the floor. A gold cord belt rested low on the hips. It was simple, but beautiful just the same. He put the dress down and picked up a dainty pair of soft slippers.

Shrewsbury grunted and nodded. Then, William picked up a metal circlet headpiece wound with silk, handmade flowers and showed it to him for his approval.

"So then, tailor," said Shrewsbury. "I will not kill you after all."

"Thank you, my lord," said William, bowing slightly. Abbey saw his legs trembling. "So am I free to go back to my home then?"

"Nay," answered Shrewsbury. "You are too good to let go. You will now start on my wedding attire."

"But, my lord," protested William with a look of horror upon his face. "The wedding is in a few hours. Surely you don't expect . . ."

"Just a simple tunic and surcoat will suffice. And perhaps I would like a headpiece as well – a crown of some sort."

"I . . . I . . ."

"Is there a problem, tailor?" he barked out.

"Of course not, my lord." William wrung his hands and stared at the floor.

Abbey could see the anxiety in William's face though his gaze was directed downward.

"Then get moving," Shrewsbury commanded. He headed

to the door and directed his next comment to Lady Bernadette. "Get Lady Abigail cleaned up and presentable. I will leave the guards at her tower door. She is not to leave until I come to collect her for the ceremony."

"Aye, my lord," said Bernadette with a curtsey.

As soon as the door closed, Abbey fell into her lady-in-waiting's arms and cried. "My brother is dead," she said. "And Madoc killed him."

* * *

MADOC DROVE the wagon into town, not caring that Barclay was at the gate, or that the townspeople stared. He stopped right out front of the church, unable to ignore the amount of people in the streets. He helped Garrett from the cart and all but carried him up the steps to the front doors. Just as he was about to enter, Dion met him at the entrance.

"Madoc, I thought I told you not to come back. The townspeople are going to cause a riot at your return." Then he looked over to Garrett, instinctively lending a hand to help the wounded man inside. "Who is this?" he asked.

"This is Abbey's brother, Garrett." Madoc spoke to Garrett next. "This is Dion, the master tailor and also a man that I consider a father in a way."

Garrett nodded his head. "Thank you for helping."

"What happened to him?" asked Dion.

"Lord Shrewsbury promised to set him free upon his marriage to Abbey, but decided to kill him instead."

"Oh, no," said Dion, shaking his head. "We cannot have fugitives claiming sanctuary in the church today."

"That is right," said a monk, coming to greet them. His

hands were hidden beneath the folds of his cape. "We are to have a wedding in a few hours and you both will have to leave. I am sorry."

Madoc looked up, first noticing the hustle and bustle inside the church as people ran to and fro placing buckets of flowers at the dais and ornate bows on the end of the benches. Red rose petals were scattered down the main aisle. He noticed several of Shrewsbury's knights conversing in the foyer. Taking a closer look, he saw that these workers were not the townspeople at all, but servants from the castle.

"God's eyes! Do not tell me this is where they plan on having Abbey's wedding?" The monk looked at him sternly. Madoc bowed his head and blessed himself for using God's name in vain in church. "Forgive me," he said. "But I just assumed Lord Shrewsbury would be getting married in the castle's chapel."

"Nay," said the monk. "He sent a messenger just this morning saying this is where he will be married."

"Abbey is not really going to marry that bastard, is she?" asked Garrett, barely able to speak.

The monk cleared his throat. Garrett glanced at Madoc in confusion. Madoc gave him a signal to bless himself for cursing, and Garrett obliged.

"She will not marry him if I have anything to do with it," said Madoc.

"What can you do?" asked Garrett. "The wedding is to take place in a few hours."

Madoc was wondering the same thing. All he knew was that he had to get back to the castle quickly. He needed to see Abbey as soon as possible to tell her he didn't kill her brother. He excused himself and was heading out the door when he spied two men carrying a woman up the stairs of the church. He almost didn't recognize his mother as she lay back in their arms, unable to walk on her own. She stared at him silently, her eyes begging him for forgiveness.

"Mother!" Madoc's hand shot out to stop the men who were carrying her. Dion ran out to join them.

"She insisted on being brought to the wedding. She is near death," explained Dion.

Madoc shook his head, not understanding any of this. "You wanted to make sure Abbey married Shrewsbury instead of me?" Disgust welled within him that his mother could be so cruel.

"Nay, Madoc," she whispered. And with her body shaking, she held her hand out to him. Madoc instinctively took it. "I want . . . to tell you . . . about . . . your past."

"I don't want to know," he told her, letting loose of her hand. "Whatever it is you have kept a secret for my entire life, I have no desire to hear it now."

"But I . . . am dying," she told him with a look in her eyes he had never seen before. "I want to tell you that . . ."

"I don't want to know," he interrupted her. Then, in the respectful manner in which he'd always treated her, he kissed her quickly atop the head. "This is my life now, and naught matters." With that, he hurried down the steps, wondering how he was going to get to Abbey.

CHAPTER 17

"*Y*ou look beautiful, my lady." Bernadette fixed Abbey's headpiece that had a small attached veil covering her face. 'Twas a symbol of virginity and purity, though Abbey knew she didn't deserve to wear it. "If only you were getting married to Madoc instead of Lord Shrewsbury today."

Abbey heard a clink and looked around the room through the veil. But she knew not from where the noise had come.

"Do not mention his name," she spat, trying to push the awful sight from her head of her brother swinging from the noose. "I never want to hear that man's name again. I hate him! Do you hear me?" she shouted, getting louder. "I hate Madoc ap Powell with every fiber of my being."

"I hear you loud and clear," came a deep voice from the window. "You don't need to shout."

Abbey and Bernadette both looked up to see Madoc hoisting himself up onto the ledge from outside, and lowering himself into the room through the window.

"Madoc!" Bernadette rushed over to look out the window, and then looked back at him. "You could have killed yourself."

"Mayhap a push would be in order?" asked Abbey snidely. "I would be more than willing to help."

Madoc pulled the rope up behind him and unfastened the four-pronged hook from the ledge that served as his anchor.

"Abbey, I need to talk to you," he said in a serious, urgent tone.

"I have naught to say to you! Now, remove yourself from here anon or I will call the guard stationed outside my door."

He moved closer to her and tried to touch her, but Abbey pushed his hands away. "Do not touch me, you murderer."

"I haven't murdered anyone yet," he told her. "However, the day is still young."

She cocked her head and looked at him through the veil covering her face. "You have the audacity to lie to my face? I saw you kill my brother with my own eyes."

"Nay. 'Twas an illusion, sweetheart. Remember, I am the *Lord of Illusion*. I wanted to tell you but couldn't. There was no time. Besides, your reaction had to be authentic in order for Shrewsbury to believe it."

"So . . . you are saying Garrett lives?"

"He is alive and hiding in the church as we speak."

"Oh, Madoc!" Abbey flipped the veil from her face and ran to him. She buried herself in his arms, then pushed away and hit him hard on the arm.

"What was that for?" he asked with a smile.

"For letting me think my brother was dead and you were a murderer."

"I am relieved, too," said Bernadette. "Can I tell William?"

"Just do not let anyone else hear," Madoc warned her.

"I must go now, my lady," she said with a curtsey. "The ladies of the castle and William need my help to finish the groom's attire for the wedding in time. If not, William may be executed."

"Not him, too," growled Madoc. "I tire of this man wanting to kill everyone he meets. I am also exhausted trying to keep up with it."

Bernadette left, and Abbey made sure to motion to Madoc to speak quietly because of the guard outside her door.

"How are you, Abbey?" he asked, concern showing in his eyes.

"My body still aches, but the swelling is going down on my eye."

He reached over then and kissed her gently on her eyelid. "I am so sorry about this. I swear I'll make that bastard pay for what he's done to you." His kiss, as well as his concern felt so wonderful that she closed her eyes, wanting it to last.

"You look beautiful in the gown William made for your wedding," he said. "I only wish that it was our wedding instead."

"As do I," she told him. "Madoc, I am very frightened. I am to marry Lord Shrewsbury in just over an hour and I don't know what to do."

"I came to help you, sweetheart." He pulled her into his arms and she willingly rested her head against his chest. Then she cried softly as they rocked back and forth in each other's embrace.

"I want to marry you, Abbey. When this is all over. I know I am only a thief and not a titled man as you deserve, but I love you and never want to let you out of my sight again. I am so sorry for all the trouble I have caused."

"I want to marry you, too, Madoc. More than anything in the world. And please do not say you are only a thief, because you are so much more to me. You are strong and brave and very romantic. You give from your heart and are even kind to animals. I do not want a man just for his title. Look at Lord Shrewsbury. He is titled, but he is the vilest, most horrible person I have ever met."

"But I may never be able to provide for you or protect you the way a knight could."

"You have already given me so much more than I could ever ask for. You risked your life many times already, and I have you to thank for saving Garrett's life."

She kissed him then, and he returned the kiss as well. She felt so safe and warm in his arms and could not help but remember the glorious time they'd spent together not long ago when both their bodies melded to one.

A knock sounded at the door. It was followed by the voice of the guard from the other side. "My lady, Lord Shrewsbury has instructed me to escort you down to the courtyard where he awaits you to take you to the church."

Abbey's heart skipped a beat. She clung to Madoc even tighter. "I cannot go," she told him. "I won't."

The guard knocked again. "My lady, did you hear me?"

"You had best answer him," whispered Madoc. "You don't want him coming in here to find me, do you?"

"I . . . I hear you," she called out to the guard, looking to Madoc for an answer. "What am I to do?" she whispered. "What is your plan?"

She watched Madoc walk to the window and look down. Then he looked over to her and picked up the rope and grappling hook and raised a brow.

"I cannot," she said, her body already shaking from the thought of descending down the rope to the far drop of the battlements below.

"Abbey, you have to."

"Nay, don't make me do it. I am too frightened by the height."

"Fine. Then go with the guard to the church," said Madoc. "I will think of another plan."

"So I am to go through with the wedding?" she asked, aghast that he should even suggest it. "This is your last chance, Madoc. If we could have just postponed the wedding for one more day, 'twould be Lent, and no priest would marry us until after Easter."

"Go, for now," he told her, kissing her once more. "I will think of something – I promise."

Madoc hid on the ground beside the bed as the guard opened the door. Abbey bit her lip and left the room with her escort, fearful that Madoc might not be able to keep his promise after all.

* * *

Madoc watched from behind the shadows of the tavern as Abbey climbed the steps to the church, holding on to the arm of Lord Shrewsbury. They were both adorned in some of William's beautiful creations. Madoc wished it were he that had Abbey holding on to his arm instead of Shrewsbury.

Lady Bernadette walked behind Abbey, straightening the back of her long gown. William followed behind her, his eyes focused on the back of the wedding couple. The lord's knights lined the stairway, holding their swords with tips together to form an arch. They walked underneath the arch of swords and stopped at the top of the stairs where the priest waited.

Abbey had never looked so beautiful, even with her bruises. Madoc felt the urgency now more than ever to try to stop this wedding from happening, but he didn't know how.

He saw Abbey looking around, probably wondering where he was. Then he looked up to the bell tower where he'd left Garrett in hiding. The man was trained well in his observations, because he spotted Madoc hiding in the shadows and acknowledged him with a slight nod.

"You are a handsome knave," came a voice, startling him. It was one of the regular whores who worked Grope Lane.

"Go away," he told her, pushing her hands from his body as she tried to feel his chest.

"I'm surprised you are not the one getting married today," she said.

"You and me both," he mumbled under his breath. "But now I need to think of a plan quickly to stop this wedding."

"Oh, you cannot stop the wedding of Lord Shrewsbury," she replied. "Not any more than you can stop the burning fire raging between my legs right now." She grabbed for him and, once again, he pushed her away. Then, he realized what she said and it gave him an idea.

* * *

ABBEY SEARCHED the room frantically for Madoc, looking into the eyes of every old woman and hooded monk as she walked down the aisle while the minstrels played a slow wedding march. Lord Shrewsbury waited beside the priest at the dais steps leading to the altar. It was customary to say their vows on the front steps and then attend the service, but Lord Shrewsbury ordered the priest to marry them inside the church instead.

A young girl scattered rose petals in front of her. Lady Bernadette followed behind her, making certain to fix her gown after every few steps. She even spotted Madoc's mother on a bench, her body leaning against the wall being supported by a town's man on either side. The man standing next to her and holding her hand, she supposed, was Dion.

The people of the town crowded in the doorway, mixed with the castle's knights and nobility as well. She was sure that the whole town of Shrewsbury attended the wedding as well as all the occupants of the castle. Everyone was here – except for Madoc.

She carried a bouquet of dried flowers since 'twas early spring. Still, she thought it fitting since the flowers were dead. If Madoc didn't stop the wedding soon, her life would be ending as well. She could not live as the wife of Lord Shrewsbury.

The bouquet in her hands shook as her body trembled in fear. She was worried that Madoc wouldn't show up in time. If not, she would have to actually marry the man who thought naught of sending her brother to the gallows. She was sure she'd be beaten on a daily basis. And she was horrified to even think of the wedding bed.

Her eyes darted back and forth, once again, looking for Madoc. She even scrutinized the priest, hoping 'twas Madoc in disguise. But to her disappointment, the music stopped and the wedding mass started as Lord Shrewsbury joined her.

They were halfway through the mass and about to say their vows, when a woman rushed into the church shouting.

"Fire! Fire!" she cried. "The town is on fire." She held up her skirts and Abbey noticed she wore no hose. By the look of her outrageous attire, Abbey was sure she was naught more than a whore. A whore in church – aye, this had to be Madoc's distraction. Only he could think of something as absurd as this.

Just then, the tower church bell started clanging, causing commotion inside the building. She could see smoke billowing outside the window, and people started running to and fro. She remembered what Madoc had told her about everyone in the town being required to assist by using the barrels of water to put out a fire.

"Let's go," someone shouted.

"We need to put out the fire," another called.

When Abbey turned to leave, Lord Shrewsbury's hand on her shoulder stopped her.

"Nay," he said. "You will stay, as our wedding is not yet completed."

"But, the town is on fire," she told him. "Surely you don't mean to continue with the wedding right now?"

The priest looked over to them with a concerned look upon his brow. He held the Bible open in front of him, but seemed like he wanted to run.

"Lord Shrewsbury," said the priest. "'Tis the duty of every person here to help put out the fire."

"Let the others do it," Shrewsbury growled. "And continue with the ceremony."

"Aye, my lord," said the priest, blessing himself and then opening the Bible once again.

* * *

MADOC WATCHED from behind the church, waiting for Abbey to run out with the rest of the occupants. When she showed up, he planned on grabbing her and heading away from here, never to return. He'd started several small fires in wooden buckets up and down the street. He figured 'twould cause enough of a commotion to stop the wedding, yet not harm anyone or burn anything of importance. He'd then sent the whore into the church and signaled Garrett in the bell tower to sound the alarm.

He waited as everyone ran out to help with the fire but, still, Abbey and Lord Shrewsbury did not emerge. He looked up to the church window and the night sky all around him. The yellow haze from the candles inside lit up the dais. He could see the priest, Bible in hand, still conducting the ceremony. He crept closer and, to his horror, he realized Abbey still stood there with Lord Shrewsbury, about to say her vows.

A wind picked up and, unfortunately, the fire spread. It caught on some of the merchants' shops. Madoc couldn't even believe this was happening. He needed to help save the town, yet he couldn't let Abbey go through with the ceremony. He bolted up the stairs of the church and dodged three people running out as he made his way frantically toward the dais.

"Stop! he shouted, just before they were about to say their vows. Abbey turned to face him, and a shadow colored her face.

"What is the meaning of this?" asked Lord Shrewsbury. "Who are you to stop our wedding?"

"I cannot let you marry the woman I love." Madoc moved closer.

Shrewsbury laughed. "And how do you think you are going to stop me?"

Obviously not worried, the man turned back toward the altar. Madoc pulled the dagger – Abbey's dagger – from his belt and quickly blessed himself in hope of forgiveness for what he was about to do. He rushed up to the altar with the dagger aimed right for Shrewsbury's back. Abbey screamed when she saw what he intended to do. Then her face paled in color. Her eyes rolled back in her head and she fell in a heap to the floor.

Madoc stopped himself from plunging the dagger into Shrewsbury. "Abbey!" He redirected his focus, dropping to his knees to be at Abbey's side. Her lady-in-waiting rushed to help. William appeared from somewhere and put his hand on Madoc's shoulder.

"What were you thinking?" William whispered.

Shrewsbury turned to realize what almost happened. He called to several of his men from the back of the church and they rushed forward and seized Madoc. As they pulled him to his feet, the dagger fell from his hand and clattered to the ground, sliding under a bench. It echoed throughout the church. The priest blessed himself and prayed aloud. Madoc knew now he'd made the wrong choice while only meaning to save Abbey.

Shrewsbury motioned for his guards to come forward. "Haul him to the dungeon," he snapped. "And make certain he doesn't escape." Then, looking at Abbey lying on the floor with her eyes closed, he cried out in anger. "Nay!" He instructed his men once more. "Throw her in the tower room and that is where she will stay for the next forty days. And make certain to guard the room."

"You can't do this," shouted Madoc, getting to his feet.

"Leave her be." A guard grabbed his hands, holding them behind his back.

Shrewsbury's fist slammed into Madoc's face and then into his stomach. "I can and I will."

Madoc released a breath from the blow and doubled over. In this situation, he couldn't even defend himself.

The monks scurried around, and the priest called out that this was a place of sanctuary, but that didn't seem to stop Shrewsbury. Of course, neither had it stopped Madoc from trying to kill the man, either.

Madoc was hauled away and dragged toward the door. That's when he saw his mother at the back of the church. Her eyes held his own pain as she sat assisted, leaning back against the wall, watching him. William followed behind him.

"Stay and take care of Mother," Madoc called over his shoulder to William. "Do not worry about me."

William rushed to his mother's side, trying to comfort her. A guard picked up Abbey's limp form and also headed out the door.

Once outside, Madoc smelled the acrid air. The fire had spread and was now consuming several of the merchants' homes as the townspeople quickly rushed to and fro with buckets of water, trying to put out the flames.

Madoc's world closed in around him. What had he done? In trying to save Abbey, he had put the entire town in danger. His good intentions had gone wrong once more. When would he ever learn? He was at the end of his bag of tricks. After what he had just done, his chances of a happy ending with Abbey were all over.

CHAPTER 18

*M*adoc fell to the dungeon floor as Shrewsbury threw him inside the cell. Then with a sickening click, he heard the cell door lock behind him.

"You will die for this stunt," came Shrewsbury's warning. "You not only stopped my wedding but now I will have to wait until the end of Lent to get married. You also tried to kill me – in a church no less."

"You beat Abbey and I will not let you get away with that," Madoc answered.

"Silence!" he shouted. "I remember your face now that I've seen it not hidden in the shadows. As well, I remember your name – ap Powell. You were the one who escaped my father's dungeon after stealing his birds. You are the only one to ever escape from the dungeon of Shrewsbury. But it will not happen again now that I am lord. You will die by my own hand the day after the morrow. I would kill you at first sunlight if it were not Ash Wednesday and a holy day."

Madoc wondered why it would even matter to the man. After all, he saw to it to pound his fist into Madoc's face right before God's eyes. Madoc would not be the only one going to hell. Shrewsbury would be right there alongside him.

"He is not to have any visitors," instructed Shrewsbury to his guard. "And make certain the girl does not leave the tower. She is now a prisoner as well."

Madoc's head snapped up at his words. Anger grew inside him once again. He might deserve to be locked away for all the wrong he'd done, but Abbey didn't. He wanted naught more than to wrap her in his arms right now and place kisses all over her body, telling her everything would be all right. But he no longer believed it. He was locked in a dungeon – again. Thrice now he found himself in this position. And this time, he had no doubt he would die here by the hands of the man who would have the woman that Madoc loved.

* * *

Abbey lay atop her bed in the tower room, her eyes popping open and fear coursing through her. She sat up abruptly, searching for Madoc.

"Madoc, nay," she cried. "Madoc where are you?" Her heart raced and anxiety coursed through her.

Lady Bernadette comforted her with a hand to the shoulder. "He is not here, my lady. You are in your chamber."

"What happened?" The last thing she remembered was Madoc rushing toward Shrewsbury with her dagger in his hand. In church. "Did he kill Lord Shrewsbury? Oh, my, this is awful. He never should have tried to kill the man in a place of sanctuary."

"He did not succeed, my lady." Bernadette handed her a

cup of ale as she spoke. "He managed to stop the wedding, but was imprisoned in the process."

"Wedding," she repeated, looking down to see she still wore the wedding gown William had crafted for her. "So I am not married?"

"Nay," she answered. "You swooned."

Now she remembered. She had faked the swoon in order to try to stop Madoc from murdering Shrewsbury. However, when she fell to the floor, she hit her head on the wooden bench, knocking herself unconscious.

"Thank the saints we stopped the wedding!" Abbey pushed the cup of ale away that Bernadette offered, and jumped to her feet. "Let me change my clothes and we will go save Madoc."

"Your door is heavily guarded, and Lord Shrewsbury instructed no one but me to be allowed to enter."

"What is going to happen to Madoc?" she asked.

Bernadette hesitated before she answered. "I am sorry, my lady, but Lord Shrewsbury plans to kill him by his own hand on the morrow."

Abbey glanced over to the window in thought. The first rays of sun broke through the sky. "So I have one day to help him."

"You cannot help him, my lady. If only there was a way to get a message to an army of men. That is what he needs to save him right now."

"Then that is what he will have," she said, with a nod of her head. "Help me change into clothes that are suitable for climbing."

"My lady?" Bernadette seemed very confused.

Abbey rushed over to the window. Thankfully, Madoc's

grappling hook and rope were still attached to the sill. She was glad he saw to leave it there after he'd left the tower. She looked down to the battlement far below and her head already dizzied.

"You cannot mean to leave the room the same way Madoc did," said Bernadette. "'Tis not safe. You could fall to your death."

"And if I do not try, then Madoc will die instead. I love him, Lady Bernadette, and I have to help him or die trying."

"I understand," she said with a slight nod. "And I will help you, because I, too, have the same feelings as you for a man. That is – for Madoc's brother, William."

* * *

WILLIAM AND DION CARRIED GWYNETH into their house and lay her on her bed to die. The smoke from the fire in town had filled her lungs. Her health was so poor, that she hadn't stopped coughing yet. With every cough, her body became weaker and weaker.

"Mother," said William taking her hands in his and kneeling at her side. "Please don't die."

"There is naught more we can do," said Dion sadly. "Her time has come and soon she will be with God in Heaven."

"Nay," she squeaked out, "I will never . . . go to . . . Heaven." She spoke in between coughs, then struggled to catch her breath.

"Do not try to talk, Mother," William said, trying to help her save her strength. But he and Dion both turned when they heard a noise at the bedchamber door. There stood Garrett, weak but able to walk, holding on to the frame of the door. He had followed them here from the church.

"You cannot come into our home," said Dion. "You are a fugitive and we are already in much danger."

"Let . . . him stay," said Gwyneth, struggling for breath.

"Mother, you don't know what you are saying," said William.

"I was wrong," she whispered. "I . . . want to help." Her eyes closed and she fell into a light slumber.

"Is she – dead?" asked Garrett from the door.

"Nay," answered William, holding her hand. "But it won't be long now."

* * *

ABBEY GRABBED on to the rope tightly, wrapping part of it around her waist the way she had seen Madoc use it. She blessed herself, took a deep breath, and scooted up to the window ledge making certain the hook to hold her weight was secure.

"Are you certain you want to do this?" asked Bernadette, wringing her hands in worry.

"Nay. The last thing I want to do is climb out a tower window, but I have no choice. I have to do it for Madoc. Now, make certain the hook does not slip once I am out the window. Then follow me yourself."

"Nay." Bernadette eyed the steep drop below with wide eyes and shook her head. "Someone needs to stay here to ward off suspicion. Besides, you might need help from someone on the inside of the castle."

"Fine then, but just don't get caught or Lord Shrewsbury will kill you as well."

Abbey had donned the hose and tunic made for a young man. Bernadette had acquired them for her from one of the servants. If she hadn't dressed this way, climbing down a rope would be out of the question. Never could she accomplish this perilous task in a gown. She also had the woman to thank for retrieving her dagger from under the bench at the church in secret. Abbey now had it fastened to her waist should she need to use it.

"Wish me luck." Abbey held tightly to the rope as she lowered her other leg over the ledge. She dangled now from the window held only by a four-pronged hook. Her body froze. Her gaze fastened down to the walkway of the battlement far below. It was void of guards and, for this, she was glad. But she no longer felt she could do this. She squeezed her eyes closed.

"Open your eyes, my lady," came Bernadette's whisper from above.

Abbey opened them, wishing this were naught but a dream.

"Now let loose a little and lower yourself down," Bernadette instructed her. "Use the knots in the rope to secure your feet."

"I can't!" Abbey's whole body shook. She wanted to go back up to the room, but found herself unable to do that, either.

"Just think of Madoc," came her lady-in-waiting's advice. "What would he say to you? Picture him in your mind."

She did just that, and felt her body relax. Abbey pictured Madoc's clear, green eyes and the way he had coaxed her up the ladder to the roof to see his birds. She envisioned his arms around her as she slowly let her grip slacken, and her body started moving toward the ground. Her fingers felt the knots randomly tied in the rope and used them to secure her feet. She moved slowly, inching her way to the walkway below. All the while, she envisioned Madoc cradling her in a protective hold as he descended with her. Everything was going fine until she heard Bernadette's warning call from above.

"Hurry, my lady. The guards knock at the door and I fear we will be discovered."

With that, anxiety coursed through her body once again. In her haste, she slipped and fell to the battlements below. Thankfully, it wasn't far. Feeling very shaken, she was relieved to know she had made her escape out the window.

"Thank you," she mouthed the words and ducked into the shadows. Now, she would just sneak out of the courtyard and make her way to town.

CHAPTER 19

*M*adoc wasn't a religious man by any means. But he found himself praying while locked away in the dungeon. He prayed not for himself, but for Abbey, so that once he was gone, she could find a way to escape the evil clutches of the man who thought to beat her.

Madoc would never think of touching Abbey in such a way. He would never touch any woman in a way that would hurt her. Lord Shrewsbury didn't deserve his title. Madoc knew a little about what was expected of a knight from the time he'd spent at Blake Castle. Chivalry was among those qualifications, and Lord Shrewsbury didn't have it.

He also prayed for William and Lady Bernadette, because he knew well by his own experience that those two could never be allowed to stay together. They were playing with fire and, hopefully, wouldn't get burned. Madoc considered William his brother, the only sibling he would ever have in this lifetime. He felt sorry for him that his masterpiece gown would never be reviewed by the guild. But William was talented. It might take a while, but he could always craft another one.

Madoc wished he had talents of his own instead of being a sad excuse for a man. It made him wonder what Abbey saw in him. He had tried to protect her and failed. Plus, he could never provide for her. She would probably see him as weak since he had never killed a man, and also failed to carry out the act of killing Lord Shrewsbury.

Most knights or titled men had seen their share of death. While heroically protecting the king and their country, they would think naught of striking down an enemy with a fatal blow. Yet Madoc had intended to kill Shrewsbury and failed. The distraction of Abbey falling to the ground had him wanting to see to her safety, pushing thoughts of murder from his mind.

"Damn!" he spat and pounded his fist against the stone wall. Pain shot through his hand and he started to bleed, but he no longer cared. Why hadn't he just killed Shrewsbury? If he had, he wouldn't be in this situation. Right now, he would be sitting down to a cold tankard of ale and some stuffed pheasant, and bedding down with the woman he loved for a night of ecstasy.

He now understood why Abbey surrendered to Lord Shrewsbury in the first place. Her brother did not deserve the inhumane way he'd been treated over the last year. But Shrewsbury thought Garrett was dead now, and Abbey no longer needed to sacrifice herself to this man. If only he could get out of here, he'd see that she got everything she deserved.

"Arrrrgh!" He pulled against the bars of the cell door angrily, shaking them until the guard shouted out for him to stop. Then he covered his face with his hands, knowing he needed one last illusion to get out of this mess. However, he hadn't a single illusion left in him anymore.

* * *

ABBEY PULLED the hood of her stolen cape over her head to hide her identity from the townspeople as she sneaked into town. Last night's fire still smoldered, sending up tendrils of smoke from the burned fronts of the butcher's shop and the chandler's shop. She could hear the townspeople talking, blaming Madoc once again for their ill fate.

It was Madoc's fault that some of them lost their shops, but she knew he had not intended for the fire to spread. He'd only intended it to be a distraction to stop her wedding. The winds picked up suddenly last night, hence the cause of the spreading fire. But these people would not see it that way.

"I hope Madoc rots in that dungeon," snarled a semi-toothless woman as she walked by.

"I hope they kill him sooner than that," snapped the butcher, sweeping up the ashes from the front of his store. Ironic, she thought. She never would have thought Ash Wednesday would have brought about ashes of a burned town.

"I hope that girl gets beaten every day from Lord Shrews-bury," said another man. "She deserves it. Madoc was never so troublesome before she came around."

This thought struck her hard. The townspeople were right. Everything Madoc had done that ended up affecting others was done on her behalf. Or most of it, anyway. Stealing her dagger had brought him trouble from the band of thieves, but that was by his hand alone.

She hurried to the tailor's shop, happy to see it had not been harmed in the fire. The pigeons cooed on the roof and she wondered if anyone had taken care of the ones that survived. She climbed the side stairs to the second floor, stopping only once to close her eyes and breathe, holding tightly to the wooden railing. She visualized Madoc there, holding out his hand to help her. After that, she was able to ascend just fine.

Abbey pushed her way into the back door to find her brother sitting at the table, eating heartily of the food a man laid in front of him.

"Garrett!" she cried out happily.

He looked up and smiled. It was something she had missed in the past year.

"Sister," he called, getting to his feet hurriedly, then held on to the table for support. He was still weak from his time in the dungeon. She ran to him and fell into his arms. They embraced and it made her so happy that she started to cry.

"I thought you were dead," she said. "I thought Madoc killed you until he told me otherwise. I am so happy to see you really did escape."

"I owe Madoc my life," he told her. "If it wasn't for him and his illusions, I would never be here right now."

"I am Dion," the man next to him announced. "So I finally meet you, Lady Abigail."

William poked his head out from his mother's bedchamber, scanning the room with his eyes. "Is Lady Bernadette with you?" he asked, the hope resounding in his voice.

"Nay," she answered. "She has stayed behind to make

excuses for my absence. I climbed out the tower window to escape."

"You did what?" asked her brother in surprise, knowing how she hated heights.

"I have Madoc to thank for my newfound strength," she said. "But right now, he is to be executed on the morrow and I need to find an army of men to come to his aid."

"Lady Abigail," said William. "My mother calls for you. She is near her time of death."

"Me?" Abbey felt confused. After all, Madoc's mother didn't like her. It was odd the woman called for her at her side at a time like this. Abbey slowly walked into the bedchamber and up to the woman, feeling nervous. When the woman saw Abbey, she tried to hold a hand out to her, but weakly put it back down. Abbey carefully reached out and held the hand of Madoc's mother, trying to comfort her the way she had seen Madoc do the day they'd first arrived here together.

"Come closer," the woman whispered. Abbey leaned forward to hear her. "Madoc loves you," she said, slowly pushing the words from her lips.

"And I love him," she reassured the woman.

"He needs to know the truth. I can . . . cannot die until . . . I tell him."

"What does she mean?" Abbey turned toward William who was watching them from the door. He came to join them at the bed.

"Tell her . . . please," the old woman whispered to William, coughing once and obviously not having the strength to say it herself.

"Lady Abigail," said William, shaking his head and wetting

his lips with his tongue. "What my mother is trying to tell you, is that it is right for you and Madoc to be together."

She looked to William in confusion. "But . . . I thought . . ."

"He is noble," came Gwyneth's whispered words. "I stole him from his family . . . as a baby."

"What!" Abbey could not believe the story coming from Gwyneth's mouth.

"'Tis true," said William solemnly. "As a young boy, I helped her steal him. Madoc's mother died giving birth and his father had left to fight for the king. The man was killed in battle."

Abbey let go of Gwyneth's hand and jumped to her feet. What kind of people were they after all? "William, you knew this secret, yet you kept it from Madoc his entire life? How could you?"

"Lady Abigail, you don't understand."

"Nay, I don't understand how two people could let a man be raised as a thief thinking he is worthless when you had the means all along to tell him of his birthright. That would have changed everything for him. All the pain he's endured because of who he is."

"They would have killed us," proclaimed William. "Besides, we lived on the run for fear Gwyneth's husband would find us and take Madoc away. He forced us to steal for him years ago. 'Twas the only life we knew. We had no choice."

"Who is this man who had you steal babies?" she asked.

"He didn't . . . that was Gwyneth's idea," William admitted. "She was never able to bear the Cap'n a baby and only wanted a family for herself."

"And so you thought to steal someone else's family?" Abbey looked toward Gwyneth. "'Tis good you never told

Madoc because he would kill you with his bare hands for your deception. Family means so much to him."

"Come . . . here," said Gwyneth, struggling to speak with what sounded like her dying breath. The woman held out her closed hand, meaning for Abbey to take the contents within it.

"What is this?" asked Abbey, picking up a small baby ring attached to a thin string made of yarn.

"'Tis the ring that Madoc's mother placed upon his arm just before she died," said William.

"Give it to . . . my son," said Gwyneth. "Tell him . . . I . . . am sorry."

Abbey looked at the ring in her hand, tracing the eagle etched upon it with her finger. "It looks like a crest," she said. "Tell me, from which castle did Madoc come?"

"Blake Castle in Devonshire," William told her.

"Nay!" Abbey's eyes opened wide, having heard Madoc speak of being at Blake Castle. "He has been spending time with the lord of the castle, and knows not that he belongs there?"

Gwyneth whispered something, and William came to her side and bent down to hear what she said. He took her hand in his as he relayed the message to Abbey. "She said they had an older brother named Corbett and a sister named Wren."

"They? What do you mean they?"

William had an expression on his face that told her she wasn't going to like what he had to say.

"There were twins," he explained. "Madoc had a twin sister, who was taken by the Cap'n."

"I cannot believe this!" she cried. Tears filled her eyes. Madoc was a titled man but would die in the dungeon thinking he was only a worthless thief. And all the time that he'd longed for a family, he had one that remained a secret all these years.

"She tried to tell him a few days ago," said William. "But Madoc didn't want to listen."

"They are going to kill him," Abbey said, looking directly at the woman on the bed. She held up the ring. "He had the means of saving himself all along. But now because of your secret, he will go to his death as a thief."

Gwyneth coughed and tried to regain her breath. Then she looked directly at Abbey and said, "Save him, please. And tell him . . . I love him." Then she released her last breath and closed her eyes forever.

"She is dead," said William, laying his head on her chest. Tears filled his eyes.

Abbey felt sad for William with his pain for the loss of the only mother he ever knew. Then she thought of Madoc locked away in the dungeon. He loved this woman. Even with the horrible deed, she was still the only mother he would ever know. Abbey longed for her own mother at a time like this. She had to help Madoc. She looked at the ring again. An eagle – a bird was etched upon it.

"I know how to help him," she said, leaving the room and rushing out the back door.

"Abigail, where are you going?" called Garrett after her.

"I am sending a message the fastest way I know how," she explained. "I am going to save Madoc."

She found a new strength within her as she climbed the ladder to the roof quickly, making her way to the pen that housed Madoc's pigeons.

"What are you doing?" called Dion, hurriedly following her up the ladder.

"I need to send out a flyer to Brynmawr right away," she explained. "I need to get a message to Owein, the man who tends to Madoc's other flock. Can you help me?"

"I can," said Dion, opening the door to the pen.

Now, Abbey only hoped that her idea would really work.

CHAPTER 20

*O*wein had just finished feeding Madoc's flock when he noticed something in the sky. A bird flew up and landed atop the pen. He could see something attached to the bird's leg and realized it was a message from Madoc.

He hurriedly made his way into the pen, able to catch the messenger bird as it dropped into the trap door. He removed the parchment tied to its leg. His son, Hadyn, walked into the coop just then and spied the note in his hand.

"What is that?" asked Hadyn.

"I'm not sure, but 'tis a message from Madoc." The parchment seemed heavier than usual, and Owein realized there was something wrapped inside. "'Tis a small ring," he observed. "With the crest of an eagle upon it."

"Let me see that." Hadyn stretched his neck to look at it. "That is the crest of Blake Castle. I've seen it when I've taken the sheep to market. There is a note with it as well."

Since neither one of them knew how to read, they had no idea what message Madoc was trying to send them.

"I told him we would take any message we received to Blake Castle," Owein relayed to his son. "Madoc said if he sent a note, 'twould be because he was in the dungeon. Take our horse and ride like the wind, Son." Owein put the message and the ring into his son's hand. "Go quickly and take the message to Lord Corbett Blake. Madoc's life may depend upon it."

Hadyn rode through the woods faster than he should have, clutching the baby ring within his fist. He hadn't gone far before he was stopped by the same group of bandits who had hurt and almost killed his father.

"Well, what have ye got for us this time?" asked the leader, riding up next to him. "Any more false information about where we can find Madoc?"

"I told you what he said last time – that he was going to Shrewsbury with the girl," answered Hadyn.

"And once there, we couldn't find him," snarled the man.

"Gruffydd," called another man from the ground. "'E's got somethin' in 'is fist that 'e's 'idin'."

Hadyn tried to slide the ring and note into his pocket, but Gruffydd's hand lashed out and grabbed it. The note fell into the folds of his cape and they did not notice.

"Well, well, a bit 'o jewelry I'd say. Just what the Cap'n likes." Gruffydd pulled it from his hand. "I spared yer ol' man's life last time, but if ye've no information to Madoc's location, I'll just kill ye instead."

"Wait," said Hadyn, trying to stop them. "I do know where he is. But please, spare my life as well as my father's. We mean no trouble. I've kept my word to tell you any information I received."

"Well, speak up then," said one of the other men. " Speak up b'fore we cut the tongue from yer mouth."

"He is in Lord Shrewsbury's dungeon," Hadyn blurted out.

"Are ye certain of this?" asked Gruffydd cocking his head. "The Cap'n will not put up with another false lead. If we find ye're lying, we'll come back and kill both ye and yer father."

"I . . . am sure," he answered, not really knowing, just guessing from what his father had told him.

"Let's go then," he commanded his men. Gruffydd turned and with one swift blow, knocked Hadyn to the ground. "Take the horse," he instructed his men. "We could use an extra one."

They rode off, leaving Hadyn sitting in the middle of the road without his horse. He reached for the parchment note stuck in the folds of his cape. He had no idea what it said, but knew it must be of great importance. The ring was gone, but he had to get this note to Blake Castle. It would be his only chance for redemption after losing the ring, and also giving them the whereabouts of Madoc twice now. He felt horrible since he really liked Madoc. But, mayhap, if he could still get word to Blake Castle in time, Madoc would not die after all.

* * *

ABBEY COULDN'T BELIEVE she was actually sneaking back into the castle. She should have stayed in town. But after she'd heard Gwyneth's confession, she knew she had to tell Madoc the truth about his true identity. The man deserved to know. If it was the last thing she ever did, she would find a way to tell him before he died.

She felt so alive sneaking through the courtyard unnoticed,

and climbing the stairs to the battlements, disappearing into the shadows as the guards focused their attention on a game of dice. The blood rushed through her. She felt the cool sting of air against her cheeks as she grabbed on to the rope that still hung from her tower window. This was the excitement missing from her life as a lady. Now she knew how Madoc felt on one of his expeditions. She welcomed the change.

After tugging the rope slightly to test that it was secure, she grabbed it high, and used her legs to straddle the rope. She then used her feet to grip the knots Madoc had tied into it, making it easier to pull herself up. It was difficult and she tried to focus on her breathing to combat her fear. It took all her strength to climb to the top. She didn't look down. Her fear of heights seemed to be diminishing since she now had a purpose. She needed to get to Madoc and naught else mattered.

Breathing heavily, arms and legs shaking from the climb, she got to the top and managed to haul herself over the ledge and drop to the floor inside the tower. Proud of herself, she knew Madoc would feel that way, too. This was an accomplishment that she never thought would happen. Brushing her hands off in her tunic, she smiled with satisfaction. But when she turned, her smile faded quickly by what she saw.

"Did you really think you would get away with this?" Lord Shrewsbury lounged back upon her bed, his arms behind his head. "Never thought I'd be able to climb the stairs to find you'd flown the coop, did you?"

"Lord Shrewsbury! I . . . I . . ." She didn't know what to say. This was truly not what she expected.

"Impressive, the way you scaled that wall," he said with a

chuckle. He sat up and scooted to the end of the bed. "Even more impressive that you came back to me."

"I did nothing of the sort," she snapped.

"Then why did you come back?" He stood and made his way over to her. "Did you think you could save your lover, Madoc?"

"He is not my lover," she said, hoping he would believe it.

"On the contrary, I heard it from a very reliable source." He shouted for his guardsman who entered the room with a struggling Bernadette in his grasp.

"Lady Bernadette?" Abbey asked in shock. "You told him?"

"I am sorry, Lady Abigail. I am so sorry." Bernadette turned her head, not able to look Abbey in the eye. Abbey gasped when she saw the bloody scratch running from the girl's chin to her ear. She knew now what had happened. Lord Shrewsbury decided to torture her until he got the information he needed.

"You bastard!" screamed Abbey, pulling her dagger from under her tunic and slashing forth, swiping it across Shrewsbury's face the same as he'd done to Bernadette.

He reached out, and iron fingers wrapped around her hand. He squeezed tightly until she was forced to drop her weapon. Then Shrewsbury kicked the dagger toward the bed and stared her in the eyes. His free hand wiped at the blood on his face that he proceeded to wipe on her hand.

"Now you have my blood on your hands and you will die for what you've done," he snarled. "I no longer want a wife who will either try to escape or kill me every time I turn my back. Take her to the dungeon," he ordered his men who filed into the room on his command. "Take them all," he shouted, motioning toward Bernadette as well. "Throw them in with the girl's lover. They will have one last night together, and then they are all going to die by my hand on the morrow!"

* * *

MADOC GOT to his feet and came to the front of the cell as soon as he heard the dungeon door open. He planned on trying to lure the guard close enough to grab his keys through the bars. He had an old spoon he'd found under the body of a dead rat near the back of the cell and he'd filed the end down to a sharp point on the stones to make a weapon should he need it. Or perhaps, he would use it to try to pick the lock.

"You are hurting me, now get your hands off me anon!" came a voice as people headed for him.

"Abbey?" He couldn't believe his ears. Sure enough, a guard opened the cell and threw her inside. He put his arms out to catch her, and pulled her warm body into his cold embrace.

"Here's another one," said yet a second guard. Madoc spied Bernadette in his grip.

"Wait," said the first. "Put her in the next cell. Lord Shrewsbury doesn't want more than two to a cell since they may try to attack us."

"They're women!" Madoc shouted. "Put her in here also."

The guard slammed the door while the other proceeded to put Bernadette in the next cell. Madoc could not see her, but heard her soft whimpers.

"What is the meaning of this?" asked Madoc, holding on to Abbey who was squeezing him tightly.

"They'll die along with you by Lord Shrewsbury's own hand on the morrow," the guard answered as he walked away. They left then, and the sound of the heavy dungeon door closing behind them seemed to Madoc to be so final. He wondered where the guard was that helped him earlier with Garrett. He really could use an ally about now.

"Abbey, sweetheart, are you all right?" He placed kisses atop her head. He noticed what she was wearing, and held her out a little to look at her.

"What did you do? Were you trying one of my attempts with a disguise?" He smiled to himself, thinking how she never failed to amuse him.

"I scaled out the window and went to town," she told him.

"You did what?" He thought he'd heard her wrong. She looked up to him, her wide eyes holding fear along with determination.

"She was so brave," came Bernadette's voice from the cell next to them. "She did it for you, Madoc."

"Abbey?" He put his hand under her chin and raised it up. "What were you thinking? You could have gotten killed."

"Madoc," she said with remorse in her voice. "Your mother is dead."

He stiffened when he heard what she had to say. His heart ached but he could not show it. He had to be strong for Abbey, and also for Bernadette. He was their protector now and would not show anything but strength.

"I will miss her," he whispered. "I wish I could go back and say goodbye to her and kiss her once more."

"She gave me a message for you, Madoc, right before she died."

"Nay," he said, holding a finger to her lips to silence her, knowing it had something to do with what his mother tried to tell him earlier. "I do not want to hear anything about my past. In a day's time, it won't matter anyway. So I will just live out the rest of my life with you in my arms."

"She loved you, Madoc," said Abbey. The look of anticipation showed in her eyes. It was evident she had something of importance to tell him, but it no longer mattered. His mother was dead and, by the morrow, he would be, too.

"I loved her, too," said Madoc. "She was my mother."

CHAPTER 21

*I*t was late in the day when Lord Shrewsbury decided to carry out the execution. Madoc had tried to pick the lock of the cell, but Abbey had been clinging to him so tightly that he had a hard time trying to do anything. Bernadette cried throughout the night, rattling his nerves and getting the other prisoners so irritated that they started shouting and calling her names.

He could have managed to lure the guard over and pilfer his keys, but he also knew he would have a hard time escaping with Abbey and Bernadette in tow. He figured he would have one last chance when he got out to the gallows. Madoc already decided he would bargain for the ladies with his own life, hoping Lord Shrewsbury would agree, therefore letting Abbey and Bernadette live.

The door to the dungeon creaked open. Madoc's stomach clenched as he heard the sound of the guardsmen coming to get them. This might be the last time he ever held Abbey in his arms. God's eyes, he loved her more than life itself. He wanted to tell her she'd be better off without him – as long as she was not in Lord Shrewsbury's care.

"I love you, Abbey. I want you to remember that no matter what happens out there."

"I love you, too," she answered. "And I cannot help but feel we are saying our last goodbyes."

He felt it, too. That this would be his last visit to a dungeon, and also the most fatal. He didn't regret meeting Abbey as she was the best thing to ever happen in his life. But he did regret the trouble he'd caused and now the innocent lives that would be lost, because he was to blame.

Three guards came forward, but something seemed different. One he recognized as Shrewsbury's guard who had helped him with Garrett. Another fumbled with the keys, while the third one looked around nervously.

"Garrett?" asked Abbey, noticing, too.

"William?" Madoc asked, looking at the guardsman who seemed the most nervous of the bunch.

"Shhh," said Shrewsbury's guard, looking back to the entrance. "I will go back to my post now to watch for trouble, but I don't know if we will get away with this. I tried my best to help you Madoc. I once worked with you in the mews years ago. I was the one who alerted Lord Shrewsbury that you were stealing. 'Tis my fault you were put in the dungeon and nearly killed in the first place. I am so sorry and only hope I can make up for it now."

"Robert," said Madoc. "We were friends. But I forgive you for what you did and thank you for helping now." Madoc first recognized Robert who he had befriended during his time at the castle. Mayhap, his past would now help his future by some twist of luck.

Robert went back to his post and Garrett finally found the right key and turned it in the lock. He opened the door and they rushed out.

"Wait – don't forget me," cried Bernadette from the cell next to them. Madoc knew they hadn't even realized she was imprisoned with them.

"Bernadette?" William rushed to her cell. He pulled the keys out of Garrett's hand and went about the task of opening the cell himself.

"Not bad," Madoc said, looking at the disguises they wore which looked exactly like the clothes of the dungeon guards. "William's handiwork?" he asked Garrett with a raised brow.

"Aye," said Garrett. "By memory, too."

"Let's get out of here," said Abbey as soon as William and Bernadette joined them. They left the dungeon, stepping over the bodies of two guardsmen at the entrance.

"Some of your handiwork, Garrett?" asked Madoc, nodding toward the guards.

"Aye," he answered once again.

Robert joined them and they hurried out into the courtyard. They may have made it to safety, but the voice of Lord Shrewsbury stopped them.

"Guards, bring the prisoners," he called to them. William and Garret froze, but Robert stepped forward in front of them.

"Aye, my lord," he answered.

Then, Madoc heard a voice he'd been avoiding for some time now.

"I want Madoc, ye can keep the rest."

"Gruffydd," grumbled Madoc, not at all happy to see the leader of the band of thieves who had been following him and causing so much trouble. As Madoc and the others approached the front gate, he realized there was no escaping. The thieves were blocking the entrance. Gruffydd's four men stood right behind him, and one was mounted on a black and white spotted horse that looked a lot like Owein's.

"Get the girls to safety," Madoc instructed William. "Just go, and do not worry about me. Keep moving, no matter what happens."

"Madoc, nay!" protested Abbey. Madoc kissed her quickly atop the head and sent her toward William.

"I will protect the women with my life, do not worry," Robert whispered back.

"Guard, bring ap Powell here at once," shouted Shrewsbury.

"Let's go," said Garrett, taking Madoc by the arm. "Robert and William can take care of the girls. Mayhap, we can think of a plan before we get up there."

"Nay," protested Madoc. "You are too weak to even think of fighting. Abbey cannot lose us both, so just go back to her, please."

"You saved my life," said Garrett talking from the side of his mouth. "Now I intend to repay the favor. Hide this somewhere." He slipped Madoc a small dagger that Madoc gratefully palmed and stashed away unnoticed.

Garrett played the part well, handling Madoc roughly, taking him to the front gate where Shrewsbury arrogantly stood awaiting their arrival.

"What do you want with him?" Shrewsbury asked Gruffydd.

"We have been trying to take him back to the Cap'n, ever since we met him. Seems he is the Cap'n's son."

That got Madoc's attention. So his father was still alive after all. And by the sound of it, he wasn't a very admirable man. Why should he be surprised?

"How do you know this is the man you seek?" asked Shrewsbury.

"We weren't sure at first, until we ran across a boy with Madoc's ring in his possession." The man held up a small baby ring that meant nothing to Madoc.

"I have never seen that before in my life," Madoc stated.

"That is a lie!" spat Gruffydd. "Ye sent it by pigeon to the sheepherder just yesterday. The Cap'n said his son's name was Madoc and that I would know him by this ring."

"Then take him," said Shrewsbury as if he didn't care. "Do to him what you would, but I never want to see him again. And you'll leave the ring for me in payment."

Gruffydd grunted and threw the ring to him. Shrewsbury caught it in one hand and perused it. Gruffydd moved forward toward Madoc, but Shrewsbury stopped him by blocking his path.

"There is a crest on the ring," Shrewsbury pointed out. "I've seen this crest before and I believe 'tis the dark lord of Steepleton's. Corbett Blake is his name. What kind of a trick is this?" He drew his sword. Madoc could hear the scraping of swords being drawn all around him. Shrewsbury didn't wait for an answer as he lunged forward toward Gruffydd. Gruffydd dodged the blow and a battle started. When Gruffydd moved toward Madoc, Garrett stepped forward with sword in hand to protect him.

Madoc readied his dagger, slipping it from his sleeve to his hand in one swift motion.

"What kind of trick is this, ap Powell?" snarled Shrewsbury. "Trying to play the thief when you are really a lord?"

"I have no idea what you mean," said Madoc. "But if I were a lord, I would have already struck you down dead."

"Kill him," Shrewsbury ordered Garrett, but Garrett was busy fighting Gruffydd. Shrewsbury raised his sword and came after Madoc.

Madoc heard Abbey screaming his name in the distance and knew this would be the last he ever heard her voice again.

Garrett, meaning to help Madoc, looked back only to have Gruffydd slash him across the cheek. He cried out and ran after Gruffydd as the thief saw to his own escape. That left Madoc standing alone with Shrewsbury.

Madoc felt so worthless. He didn't even have a weapon other than the dagger. It wouldn't matter. He'd be dead in seconds anyway, and only regretted that Garrett would be dead along with him. He only hoped Robert could get William and the women to safety so they would not suffer the same fate.

"Nay!" shouted Madoc, in what he knew would be one of his final words. "I will kill you, you bastard, if it is the last thing I ever do."

With that, he rushed forward, seeing his life pass before his eyes. As if in slow motion, he met with Lord Shrewsbury in a deadly battle. Madoc's quickness and lithe alone managed to avoid the end of the man's sword. He then was able to knock the man off balance because of his bad leg. And then, in all his anger and rage for what the man did to the people he loved, Madoc jumped atop Shrewsbury and plunged his dagger straight into the man's heart, over and over again.

He'd barely noticed the sound of hoofbeats and the shouting and clashing of swords all around him. He waited for the tip of a sword to pierce his back at any moment, but it never came. He pulled the dagger from Shrewsbury's chest, blood dripping down his arm. He'd killed his first man. It was an empowering feeling because he loathed the man so much but, at the same time, he felt as if he'd done something horribly wrong. He knew from this day on, he would never be the same.

"Madoc!" Abbey screamed his name, pulling away from Robert's protection. When Madoc turned around, she barreled into his embrace. He dropped the dagger and wrapped his arms around her, burying his face in her hair.

That's when he saw Lord Corbett Blake and his men from Blake Castle in the courtyard, fighting and taking the rest of Shrewsbury's men as prisoners. William rushed up with Lady Bernadette, without his disguise. Garrett pulled his sword from a dead man, tearing off his disguise as he, too, came to join them.

"Gruffydd managed to escape," Garrett informed them. "But the rest of his men are dead." He looked over to Madoc and then to Shrewsbury's dead body on the ground. "Your handiwork?" he asked with a raised brow.

Madoc silently nodded.

Lord Corbett gave his men orders to carry out, and dismounted his horse and approached Madoc's side.

"Lord Corbett, what are you doing here?" asked Madoc.

"We met a young man on the road who happened to be heading to Blake Castle. He gave me your message you sent by pigeon. I am only glad we got here before they killed you – Brother."

Corbett smiled, but Madoc truly had no idea of what he meant.

"'Twas me who sent the missive," Abbey said, looking up at Lord Corbett. "I am Lady Abigail of Blackmore." Then she looked back to Madoc. "'Twas what I was trying to tell you, Madoc. Your mother's last wish was for me to tell you that she stole you as a baby. And that you are of noble blood."

Madoc could not comprehend what he was hearing. How could he be a thief one day and a lord the next? And how could a woman he had loved and called mother have lied to him his entire life?

"William?" Madoc looked at his brother. "Did you know about this?"

"I am sorry, Madoc. I wanted to tell you. But Gwyneth loved you like a son. And her secret exposed would mean the death – of both of us for what we'd done."

"The ring your mother gave me is proof that you are Corbett's brother," Abbey interjected. "I attached it with a note to one of your birds and sent it to Owein."

Madoc walked over to Shrewsbury, pulling the small ring from the grip of the dead man. He wiped it off on his tunic and held it up for all to see. "This ring?" he asked, seeing the crest of Lord Corbett engraved upon it.

"It was tied onto your wrist as a baby," William offered the information. "As was another ring on the wrist of your twin sister."

Madoc shook his head. This was more than he could comprehend. "Twin sister?" He looked to Corbett for confirmation.

"Aye, Brother," Corbett said, smiling. "You have two sisters. Wren, and your twin who was stolen the same time as you."

"Her name is Echo," William told them.

Corbett bit his lip and shook his head. "For all these years, I thought you were dead." Then he pushed forward and wrapped one arm around Madoc, slapping his back with the other as he pulled him into a tight embrace. Madoc did not know what to say.

"What will happen to William?" asked Madoc, looking over at the man who he once considered a brother.

"Sadly, he will have to be brought to trial," said Corbett. "Stealing noble babies is not taken lightly." Corbett instructed his men to seize William, causing Lady Bernadette to cry out.

"Please," said Madoc. "Can it at least wait until after we bury my . . . Gwyneth?"

"Aye," Corbett answered. "I will do that for you. Brother."

CHAPTER 22

The next morning, Madoc stood solemnly, hands crossed in front of him as his mother's body was lowered into the ground behind Shrewsbury's tavern. Abbey stood at his side, as well as his newfound brother, Lord Corbett Blake of Devonshire. William walked forward and threw a handful of dirt atop the wooden casket Lord Corbett had so generously provided. They were not allowed to bury the woman in or near the church because of the horrible things she had done. Madoc thought it only right she be buried near Grope Lane where the poor and the people of questionable nature were laid to rest.

"Madoc, 'tis your turn," said Abbey with a slight tug to his sleeve.

He bent down and scooped up a handful of dirt and moved forward and released it over her casket. "I forgive you, Mother," he said softly, knowing no matter what horrible deeds she had done, he'd always have a special place for her in his heart. She was the only mother he had ever known. And as Corbett had explained, both his true parents were dead.

He stood there staring, not able to move. Abbey went to him and gently pulled him back as the gravediggers buried Gwyneth's casket beneath the cold earth. There was no mass for a poor woman of deceit. No prayers or kind words spoken. Just a hole in the ground where her body would rot and her soul would probably go to places he didn't want to think about. It was exactly where Madoc felt he should be along with her for some of the things he had done.

"Madoc?" Abbey pulled him from his thoughts. "Everyone is going to your house where Dion has prepared a meal. Let us join them."

Dion had said his goodbyes to Gwyneth earlier in private, not able to watch the woman he loved being lowered into the ground. He heard the story of Gwyneth's husband who was still alive and nothing more than a thieving pirate that the bandits called Cap'n. That was why Gwyneth refused to marry him like he'd begged her to for so many years.

Madoc wrapped his arm around Abbey, never wanting to let her go. They strolled back to Dion's house – the house that had also been Madoc's home. He saw the booths being set up in the street and the people registering who would compete in the pigeon race shortly. He had been so excited about it at one time but, now, he had no passion for it left within him.

"What's the matter, Madoc? You seem so quiet. 'Tis not like you," remarked Abbey.

"I'm sorry," he said. "'Tis just that so much has happened in the last day."

"I understand. But you do like the fact that you are a titled man, don't you?"

"I do," he told her. "Although I am not sure I deserve it

since I have done many questionable things in my life that are not to be admired. And I know I don't deserve you."

She stopped and looked at him. "Are you saying you no longer want to marry me?"

"Not at all," he answered. "I want that more than anything in the world. And once Easter is here and marriages are once again allowed, we will be married, I promise."

"You do realize, no coupling is allowed during Lent either. Unless you want to go against the rules of the church."

"You know I do," he said with a smile. "However, if you would be willing to wait, I think I would like to start living a better life first. Anything I can do to get back in God's good graces would probably be a wise move."

'Twas her turn to laugh this time. "I, too, need all the grace I can get. Especially from my father. So until we hear from him, I do think 'twould be wise to hold back our appetites a little."

He pulled her into his arms and kissed her deeply. His loins stirred for her and he already regretted the deal with God he'd just made. "We had better go eat and take care of our other appetites as well," he told her, kissing her once again. "I can only hope I won't starve before Lent is over, in more ways than one."

"Madoc, Madoc!"

Abbey heard the call and saw Owein rushing over to them holding a wooden cage with a bird inside.

"Owein?" asked Madoc. "What are you doing here in Shrewsbury?"

"I found a vendor coming this direction and rode here as fast as I could with Homer. I just hope I am not too late for ye to get into the pigeon races."

"You are a good man, Owein." The smile was back on Madoc's face when he took the cage with his favorite pigeon from Owein. Abbey was glad, as she'd been very worried about Madoc. Ever since yesterday when so much of his life changed so fast, he had been acting odd.

"Hadyn is waiting for the release of the bird. He will bring it as fast as he can on horseback once the bird returns to the pen in Brynmawr. Hopefully, ye will have the fastest time and win the race."

"Hadyn is a fine lad to do this for me," said Madoc.

"Not as fine as ye think. The thieves forced him to tell them yer whereabouts. He only did it because they'd threatened to kill me if he didn't."

"I hold no grudge toward him," Madoc explained. "He did what he had to in order to protect his father. I admire him for that."

"Well, 'tis the least he can do to make up for the trouble he's caused. Now, let's get over to the booths to register, as they are getting ready to release the pigeons for the race soon."

"Aye," said Lord Corbett walking up to join him. "And I will vouch for you that you are now nobility and have every right to race the bird for the prize money."

After a short meal at the house and showing his new brother, Corbett, what was left of his flock atop the roof, Madoc stood waiting in a straight line with Homer held securely in front of him. All the competitors stood waiting to release their flyers. Although Madoc only had the one, he still felt proud to be a part of the competition.

"So if all the birds go back to their own roosts," asked

Bernadette, watching from the side with the rest, "then how do they know who won?"

"I think I can answer that," said Abbey proudly, having asked Madoc the same question earlier. "They are timed from where they are released, to the distance of their home, and the time it takes someone to ride back here with the pigeon in hand."

"The pigeons in the race are all marked with a certain ribbon," William added.

"True," added Owein. "That way, they know 'tis truly the bird that entered the race."

"And what is the prize?" asked Garrett.

"That, I can answer," said Dion. "The man of the winning bird will take home a gold florin."

"That's quite a sum to place on the head of a bird I've often eaten for dinner," Corbett said with a chuckle.

"Do not let your new brother hear you say that," warned Abbey. "He has taken quite a liking to pigeons."

A bell rang to signify the contestants should ready their birds. Madoc kissed Homer on the head and looked into her two-toned eyes. "Do me a favor, and win," he whispered.

He planned on using the prize money to make repairs to the town he'd about burned down, not to mention repay Dion for the supplies he'd lost. Madoc wanted to right the wrongs in his life, and knew 'twould take a lifetime to do it.

The second bell sounded, and Madoc threw the bird up into the air to release it. With a few flaps from her wings, Homer took off in flight over the vast skies along with all the other birds. It was one of the most beautiful things Madoc had ever seen. The sky was filled with all these birds flying back to their homes.

Abbey came to him then and wrapped her arms around his waist. He sheltered her body with his to keep her from the cool, spring breeze.

"When will they know the results of the race?" she asked him.

"The birds will return to their homes shortly. But we will have to wait until the morrow for their return back to Shrewsbury. We should know by first light."

"Madoc," said Corbett, "I would like to talk to you about William."

"Aye," Madoc answered. But instead of sending Abbey away, he kept her at his side.

"You know that what he did by stealing you as a baby is punishable by death."

Madoc looked over to William who was laughing, with Bernadette clinging to his arm.

"He was the only brother I knew for my entire life up until yesterday," said Madoc. "And though he was an accomplice to my mother's crime, he did not have a choice."

"And don't forget, he did help in Madoc's escape," Abbey so eagerly pointed out.

"Aye," added Madoc. "If it hadn't been for his tailoring the things we needed, we might all be dead right now."

"So is it your wish he be spared from trial and punishment?" asked Corbett.

"Aye," said Madoc eagerly. "I wish that he could be granted the opportunity to live his life as a free man. I am sure his guilt will imprison him until the day he dies."

"Then, little brother, that is how it shall be. I will tell him at once that he is free. However, he will not ever be allowed to step foot into Blake Castle or even in all of Devonshire for the rest of his life."

"Thank you, *big* brother," Madoc said jokingly. "But if you ever call me *little* again, you may have your first brotherly fight."

"I don't believe you even know how to fight or use a weapon," Corbett said with a smile. "But I will take it upon myself to teach you the ways of a knight as soon as we return to Blake Castle."

"'Tis appreciated," said Madoc with a nod.

Corbett walked away, and Abbey looked up to Madoc. "Where should we live when we get married, lord husband?" she asked. "Will we have our own castle for you to rule? I am sure my father could arrange for us to live in Shrewsbury."

"Nay. There are too many bad memories here for me to stay. I would like to live at Blake Castle with my new family. Lord Corbett . . . my brother, has said we are welcome there."

"Then that will be our new home. And what of your training as a knight?"

"I will take up my brother's offer. And I will act as is expected of a man who holds my title, now. But Abbey – I killed my first man, and I cannot say I am proud of it. Still, I need to be able to protect you and the family we will have someday. I must also protect my king and country. But I do not know if I'll ever feel at ease with a weapon in my hand. After all, I have really only been trained to be one thing in this lifetime, and that is a thief."

CHAPTER 23

EASTER, BLAKE CASTLE

*M*adoc sat at the dais table next to his new wife, feeling like the luckiest man in the world. He and Abbey had been married early that morning and then attended the Easter mass, given by Father Chapman in St. Basil's Cathedral. Madoc's brother, Corbett, had stood next to Madoc and handed him the beautiful gold and diamond rings that Madoc bought with some of the prize money he'd won thanks to Homer winning the race.

He'd slipped the ring onto Abbey's finger while saying the poetic vows he'd written for her. Thankfully, through his nervousness he'd remembered his words and hadn't started spouting nonsense like he'd done once before.

William's present to Abbey had been the beautiful wedding dress she now wore. Madoc was only sorry that his surrogate brother had been banned from Devonshire as William would have loved to see Abbey wearing it. It was even more elegant than the one he'd made for her the first time, and the craftsmanship was superb.

By Abbey's choosing, and the expected color of a noble's wedding gown, he'd crafted her a dress in a light blue crushed velvet, interspersed with shiny, white satin.

A square neckline was dotted with dainty, white, embroidered roses. The long sleeves were trimmed part way down with lace, and the tight sleeves underneath went past her wrists and down to her fingers as was the style. White tippets angled down from her elbows to the ground. The bodice closed with a crisscross of satin ties that pulled together her breasts, showing off her cleavage – Madoc's present from William. He'd have to thank him later.

On her feet were slippers of satin. Her headpiece was a beautiful metal circlet with sapphires and diamonds – a gift from her absent father who was on a mission for the king but would visit with them soon. He had heard of their troubles in Shrewsbury, but was elated to have Madoc marry his daughter since he had saved Garrett's life.

Fresh, small periwinkles and lush, green ivy were braided into Abbey's hair with blue and white satin ribbons that wound up into a spiral atop her head. A long, white veil trailed down her back, with tiny pearls stitched into the lace. Her wedding outfit was such a masterpiece that it had earned William the title of master tailor from the guild.

Dion ended up leaving Shrewsbury, selling his shop to William at a very reasonable price as his wedding present to William and Bernadette who had decided to get married. Madoc was able to repay Dion for all he'd lost, and also to fix all the shops in Shrewsbury that had burned because of him.

"Wife, you look ravishing." Madoc looked over to her

smiling face and raised the wedding cup filled with spiced wine in a toast. "To the most beautiful wife and the luckiest man alive," he said. Cheers went up from the crowd and everyone raised their cups into the air. Madoc handed the cup to Abbey and drank from it after she'd finished.

"Madoc, this is the happiest day of my life," said Abbey, smiling at him and then turning to Wren, Madoc's newfound sister, seated next to her along with her Scottish husband, Storm. "And I am so happy to meet you, Wren. I thank you for acting as my bridesmaid today and for the beautiful bouquet you've created for me."

"'Twas my pleasure," said Wren. "Besides the wildflowers in your bouquet, I've included sage to symbolize strength and wisdom, thyme for courage, and rosemary to symbolize your faithfulness to each other as well as remembrance and the love between you. And, of course, a little wheat to ensure fertility," she added with a smile.

"Aye," agreed Storm. "Wren should ken about that since we are bairned."

"You're having a baby! Congratulations," said Abbey.

"Losh me," Storm continued. "Enough of this clish-maclaver, now let's eat. I havena had meat in forty days and my achin' body is weak."

"Storm, you've had fish during Lent," said Wren. "So don't act as if you are going to die of starvation. And now you know how it feels to never eat meat, just like me."

Abbey laughed at the Scotsman and his unsubtle ways. She, too, was hungry since during Lent no meat or dairy was allowed to be consumed. A bowl of hard-boiled eggs dyed in colors of saffron and purple from boiled onion skins and wine, sat in a centerpiece before them. Madoc grabbed one and Abbey playfully slapped his hand.

"What did I do wrong?" he asked.

"Those are to be given to the mummers in pay for the skits and entertainment they will provide. Besides, there are games planned with them later, and even an egg dance. Some will be hidden for the children to find."

Madoc shook his head and replaced the egg with the rest. "You will not see me doing an egg dance, Wife."

"Madoc," said Corbett, overhearing the conversation. "I would venture to say you will be doing many new things during your life at the castle. And though I will not be teaching you the egg dance, I will see to your training personally in the ways of weapons of war."

"Aye," said Madoc. "And I could teach you a few ways of creating illusions if you should ever need one, Brother. Like disappearing when it's time to dance with eggs."

They all laughed as the feast was laid before them.

"I hope you are not against the idea of eating peacock," said Lady Devon as a serving wench laid before them a full peacock to which the plumage had been reattached. Madoc looked over to the ornate bird in awe. He'd never seen anything like it while living the life of a peasant.

"Just as long as there will be no pigeons served at our wedding feast, I will agree to try anything," Madoc said willingly.

Father Chapman said the prayer for the meal and the musicians started up their cheery tunes. Mutton, rabbit and wild boar were placed before them as well as dishes with parsnips and several other vegetables. White bread – reserved for the nobles – was served along with small earthenware jars containing herbed garlic butter. Madoc had never seen anything like it in his life.

When next they laid something down in front of him, he had no idea what it was. Abbey must have seen the bewildered look upon his face since she took it upon herself to explain.

"'Tis black pudding – made from the blood of the animals we are to consume," she explained. "'Tis very tasty."

"Abbey," he told her. "At one time, you had never seen a town, and now I have much to learn about my new life at the castle as well."

"I only wish my father could have joined us," said Abbey. "However, he will have a special celebration for our marriage when we visit him at Blackmore Castle soon. Still, I do miss him, though I am happy to have my brother, Garrett, with us."

"Did I hear my name mentioned?" asked Garrett, walking up to the table with a tankard of ale in his hand. A scar ran across his cheek from his fight with Gruffydd. Garrett had sworn he would hunt the man down for what he'd done if it took him the rest of his life.

"Madoc," said Garrett. "I just found out from Lord Corbett that you used most of your prize money from the pigeon races to help the people of Shrewsbury."

"Aye," Madoc answered. "I do believe the town no longer hates me, and actually welcomes me back."

Madoc spied Owein across the room and motioned to him with his hand to come forward. Madoc nodded to him and approached the dais.

"Owein has a wedding present for you, my beautiful wife," Madoc explained to Abbey.

"Aye, my lady," Owein said with a slight bow.

"You do?" asked Abbey, looking at Madoc suspiciously.

"Hadyn will be in charge of my birds in Brynmawr from now on," Madoc explained. "The boy wants to start racing them, and I will be training him. He will be my communication with William in Shrewsbury, where he will watch over my other pen."

"What about Homer?" she asked. "You didn't get rid of her, did you?"

"Nay, I couldn't. I brought her here to start a new pen. But Owein thought Homer would be lonely." He nodded, and Owein handed Abbey a box. She opened it and two beautiful doves flew out, surprising her so much that she grabbed on to Madoc's arm. Madoc laughed and wrapped his arm around her shoulder.

"They are some of Madoc's fledglings," Owein explained. "This will be their new home now."

The birds flew up to the ceiling rafters. Storm's Scottish Deerhound, Mools, darted out from under the trestle table. The hound knocked into a serving wench who fell to the rushes with a tray of food in her hand. Two more hounds darted out to lick up the food.

"Catch those birds," came Heartha, the head cook's cry from the corridor. "They'll make a good meal now that Lent is over."

"Nay," shouted Madoc. "You cannot eat my wife's wedding present."

"Don't harm the birds," shouted Wren, getting up out of her chair. "Storm, do something."

Abbey noticed Lord Corbett holding on to his trencher, and knew why as soon as the Scotsman cleared the table with one swipe and jumped atop it. "Dinna worry, I will get the birds."

"Not again, Madoc!" shouted Corbett, holding tight to his food. "If you are going to be living here, from now on you leave your pets in the mews or I swear I will give the order personally to put them on the table for dinner."

Madoc took this opportunity to rush Abbey out to the corridor in the midst of the commotion. They ran out laughing, watching everyone scurrying around trying to catch the birds. Wren's son, Renard, had brought his pet fox into the hall. Once the fox was loose, the hounds started up the chase. The musicians stopped playing, and women held up their skirts as the knights gallantly tried to protect their ladies from the havoc.

"Do you think we should try to catch them?" asked Abbey.

"Do you mean the doves or the wild Scotsman and his mischievous son?" answered Madoc with a chuckle. They both laughed and Madoc continued. "Nay. Owein will collect the doves. They are not in any danger."

He pulled her into the shadows and kissed her then. Abbey felt the most glorious feeling to be Madoc's wife.

"I have something for you, Abbey." Madoc pulled her dagger from his waist belt. The pink and green gems glittered in the torchlight from the hall. "Lady Bernadette found it in the tower room after we left Shrewsbury Castle. William sent it over by messenger. And I don't mean the birds."

"So I finally get my dagger returned," she said with a smile. "I sure had to go through a lot to get it."

"I am sorry for ever taking it in the first place," he told her. "And I know how much it means to you because of the fond memories of your mother. But this dagger is what brought us together, and I wouldn't trade that for the world."

"Leaving the celebration so soon?" Orrick, the old sorcerer, walked out from the shadows.

"Old man," said Madoc. "You were right when you said I would be here with my family someday. I never should have doubted you."

Orrick's amethyst eyes twinkled. He looked out to the great hall. "Not all of your family is here yet."

"What does he mean?" asked Abbey.

"Have you seen something in your crystal ball about possibly someday finding my twin sister?"

"That depends. What can you tell me about that man dancing with Zara?" Orrick asked. "The one with the scar on his face."

Madoc looked out to the great hall to see Garrett, well in his cups, dancing with the old gypsy, Zara. "That is Abbey's brother, Garrett."

"He will be going on a journey soon," said the sorcerer. "It will take him far across the water."

"Oh, I doubt it," said Abbey. "He has been imprisoned so long he will probably be happy to head home."

"One thing I've learned is to never doubt the sorcerer," said Madoc. Orrick nodded wisely and left them, heading out to the great hall. Then Madoc bent over and whispered into Abbey's ear, "Are you ready for me to take you to our wedding bed, Wife?"

Abbey's heart raced as she thought of the last time they'd coupled. It had been so long ago that she could hardly wait to do it again.

"I am," she said in eager anticipation of once again being in Madoc's arms.

"Then you will wait no longer." He swept her off her feet and headed down the corridor toward their solar.

"Shouldn't we wait until after the celebration?" she asked.

"I will wait no longer to consummate our marriage. I might be a lord now but, deep down, I will always be a thief. And right now, I plan on stealing your heart."

"You stole my heart long ago," she assured him. "But I look forward to whatever else you have planned for me. And I will love you forever, Madoc, my *Lord of Illusion.*

FROM THE AUTHOR

I hope you enjoyed **Lord of Illusion**, Book 3 in the **Legacy of the Blade Series**.

Madoc and Abbey had minds of their own, and while writing their characters, I found that not every hero in medieval times has to be a master at wielding the sword. Madoc had a whole other layer about him that I was surprised to encounter. It was brought out by the fact that he'd been raised by a single mother with no real male role model in his life. What a man lacks in physical prowess he makes up for with intellect and lithe. Abbey, too, was a surprise for me, as I normally embrace the tougher, independent side of my heroines. It was nice for me to see more of a lady - though still feisty - from the start.

I also wanted to bring in the flavor of living in a town, and show how the masters at their crafts tried hard to join the guilds. Men dominated the trades in this time period, so it was common for a man to be a tailor.

The next and final book in the series is **Lady of the Mist**,

Book 4. Echo, Madoc's twin sister, is far from a lady, having more of the pirate blood running through her. The hero of the next book you have already met – Abbey's brother, Garrett. He is a baron of the Cinque Ports, protecting the channel from pirates – or Echo! In case you missed Book 1, **Lord of the Blade,** or Book 2, **Lady Renegade**, you may want to catch up on what happened earlier. And be sure to pick up a copy of the **Prequel** .

If you enjoyed my **Legacy of the Blade Series**, you may want to try my medieval **Daughters of the Dagger Series**. You will find some guest appearances by some of the characters from **Legacy of the Blade** crossing over into that series.

Thank you,

Elizabeth Rose

ABOUT ELIZABETH

Elizabeth Rose is a multi-published, bestselling author, writing medieval, historical, contemporary, paranormal, and western romance. Her books are available as EBooks, paperbacks, and audiobooks as well.

Her favorite characters in her works include dark, dangerous and tortured heroes, and feisty, independent heroines who know how to wield a sword. She loves writing 14th century medieval novels, and is well-known for her many series.

Her twelve-book small town contemporary series, Tarnished Saints, was inspired by incidents in her own life.

After being traditionally published, she started self-publishing, creating her own covers and book trailers on a dare from her two sons.

Elizabeth loves the outdoors. In the summertime, you can find her in her secret garden with her laptop, swinging in her hammock working on her next book. Elizabeth is a born storyteller and passionate about sharing her works with her readers.

Please visit her website at **Elizabethrosenovels.com** to read excerpts from any of her novels and get sneak peeks at covers of upcoming books. You can follow her on **Twitter, Facebook, Goodreads** or **BookBub.** Be sure to sign up for her

newsletter so you don't miss out on new releases or upcoming events.

Cowboys of the Old West Series

And more!

Please visit http://elizabethrosenovels.com

Elizabeth Rose

Made in the USA
San Bernardino, CA
17 March 2020